Stuart An[...]

By

Mj Ebdell

The comical, strange, and occasionally sad, but mostly funny,
story of three English
people stuck in a house in Spain, with several cats,
for the first Lockdown of 2020.

Copyright © 2021 Mj Ebdell
All rights reserved.

CHAPTER ONE

I packed my suitcase then cleaned my teeth and got into bed. And, as I lay there, I thought about it. I thought about those four small wheels and how hard it would be to move the case over the cobblestones to the bus stop. And I thought about the noise it would make, echoing in the silent streets of the early morning. Then I wondered how humanity had managed to put a man on the moon in the 1960's but waited another fifty years before thinking of putting wheels on suitcases. Then I thought about picking the case up and carrying it, and about the wrist I had broken a few short months ago, which immediately began to ache and remind me that I am way passed my prime. I got out of bed and emptied the case. After all, it's Spain, why would I need jeans and trainers, why would I need more than two cardigans, why would I even need socks? I only needed what I could fit into my small back pack. No luggage to check in or wait for at the other end. That had to be better. I was only going for two weeks after all.
If only I had known.

I had been devastated when my beloved van had broken down less than half way through my trip. At first I could see no way out other than to ship it home, but then I had thought about Raymond. Hidden away in a tiny Portuguese village, only taking on jobs he wanted to do and working alone, I considered him to be the best mechanic in Europe. As honest as Richard, the man who looked after my van back home in Cornwall, and about half the price. So I had called him and told him the problem.
"Do you think you can fix it?" I had asked.
"It's a Merc," he had said, "Of course I can fix it."
So I had paid a local man to come and pick it up and take it to Raymond's village on the back of his recovery truck.

Raymond had said it would take him about two weeks to strip down the engine, fix the problem and put it back together again. He had been happy for me to stay inside it, inside his garage, using his shower and his wifi, while he worked on it, but I had known that I would be bored senseless there. Raymond is the only person in the village who speaks English and my Portuguese is restricted to 'Obrigado' or nodding my head because I cannot get used to saying Sim instead of Si. He may be the only mechanic in Europe I truly and honestly trust, but his village, miles away from anywhere, is boring. I had spent three weeks there before and had just about coped. But I had had my lovely little dog with me then, and had been happy to spend time wandering around the place with him. But Nipper had not made it home from our previous trip. I had had to let him go over that rainbow bridge and now I was travelling alone.

So, not wanting to spend the next two weeks utterly alone I had contacted Ruth in Spain and asked if I could stay a couple of weeks, and she had responded with "Yes, of course, it will be lovely to see you. Just let us know when to pick you up."

The only bus out of the village was the school bus and it left at seven in the morning so as to get the kids to school by eight. It was the main reason I needed to travel on a weekday; because if there was no school there was no bus and it was a five kilometer walk to the patch of flattened earth that served as a stop in the nearest railway line. The trains ran every day, but only once a day. At a similar time. Sort of.

There were only two children in the village who were old enough to go to senior school and both of them knew me by sight. Or at least they knew about the strange foreign woman with the yellow van that shows up now and again, and who pushes an elderly dog about in a pram. They both nodded a good morning and went back to their phones.

I wasn't quite the oldest person on the bus; there were a couple of tiny ladies with headscarves and shopping bags and the driver looked to be at least 101. Although I did think that the guy in the police uniform looked very young. Oh gods, that's a sign of getting old isn't it? Wondering if the policemen are old enough to leave school? I stayed on past the school and the policeman didn't get off so I had to accept that he was real and I was possibly getting old. Then we reached Portalegre bus station where I got off and bought a ticket for Lisbon. It seemed like an odd thing to do; taking a bus right across the country just to get a plane back again and I wondered if I could have flown from Badajoz. But it was too late by then, my flight was booked.

The airport was the first place I saw people wearing medical face masks. Some did, some didn't. I was in the 'didn't' group as I was still wondering if it was really worth the panic. But I did have hand sanitizer.
This is something I had carried for a few years anyway. I'm not the sort of person who can show my finger tips to a dripping tap and call it a wash, and so many public toilets don't have soap or paper towels, or even running water (or even toilets in some countries, but that's another story). I have found hand sanitizer to be a handy thing to carry on my travels.
 And in my winter shop.

After spending the summers working outside I spend three months of each winter running a shop where I come into contact with not only the sickness inducing fan heating, but also all sorts of bugs and germs that are coughed on me and thrive in that warm environment. The first three winters I became quite ill during the first few weeks, but then I discovered hand sanitizer and a wipe off cleaner for my shop's counter. Once I had started using them and keeping my distance from anyone who looked like they might cough or sneeze over me, I stopped being ill. Yes, this was all in the years BC. (Before Covid) and I was already well known for telling people who claimed to be ill to "Please keep back, I don't want to catch it."
So I had some sanitizer with me that day. Well, at least I did for part of that day.

My bottle was almost empty but it said 200ml on the outside and the rules are no liquids of more than 100ml on the plane. As I only had about 50ml in the bottle I thought it would be ok, that their x-ray machine would pick up on its contents and I would be allowed to keep it.
I thought wrong.
The box my bag was in was dragged from the x-ray machine by a stern looking woman of about fifty who then stood with her hand on my bag while looking over the top of her glasses at the people shuffling past. I tried to politely attract her attention by waving and saying "That's mine."
She walked to the end of the conveyer belt and slid the box onto the rack next to it so I could reach it from the other side.
"Open." She said. I was more of a command.
Believing I had done nothing wrong and had nothing to hide, I did so. She reached her hand in, took out the bottle of sanitizer and simply began to walk away with it.
"Excuse me!" I said.
She returned to face me holding out the bottle in front of her.
"Is too much," She said.

"But there's only about 50 mil left"
She pointed to where it said 200ml and told me that the limit was 100ml.
"But there isn't even 100mil left." I said. She shook her head and went back to her machine. I had been dismissed. Silly cow, I thought, I'll get some more on airside.
No, actually I wouldn't. Because there was none left on the shelves. The panic had begun. If only people had been this clean before!

My flight to Madrid was uneventful and I spent it mainly in the company of Lee Child's Jack Reacher. But once off the plane I found I had to run, and I'm really getting too old for running, to get to the other side of the airport to get my connecting flight to Alicante. There were no restrictions at that point and I arrived, sweating and panting, to find my fellow passengers crowding around the gate looking like one of those cartoon video clips that show downtrodden depressed people patiently waiting to walk thought a funnel into a mincing machine. Eventually they were moved into some sort of line by two rather handsome uniformed men and, just as I was wondering what I could get myself arrested for, I saw the sign change. The flight was going to be late leavening.
I found a seat, and fell asleep.
I awoke to find one of the aforementioned men prodding me and then pointing to the gate which was just about to close. I didn't even have time to worry if I had been snoring or dribbling as I slept, I just ran.
An hour and a half later I was at Alicante Airport where I walked past the queue of people waiting for their luggage to do a full circuit before recognizing it, and out of the door with my single carry-on bag luggage, to the main airport where I found Stuart and Ruth waiting for me.

I had first met Ruth when we worked together in Cornwall. I had found her to be a bit bossy, but she was nice in other ways, and we got on quite well. At that time she and Stuart were in England working to pay a debt on their house in Spain. Had things gone according to plan they should have been quite comfortable for the rest of their lives once they moved out there around the turn of the century. But things rarely go according to plan, and when things went wrong for Europe things went really wrong for Stuart and Ruth and they had to return to the UK to find work to pay the debt. After about five years they had paid it off and gone home once more to Spain and now lived on his pension.

I had been to their house once before, a couple of years previously, but only because I didn't want to go to Benidorm. Usually when driving around the Spanish coast I avoid Benidorm at all cost. I will head inland for a bit and get back to the coast once passed what I consider to be the British hellhole. My claim to fame used to be that I have been to Athens eleven times and never seen the Acropolis, now it is that I have been to Spain eight times, driven right around the south coast three times, and never been to Benidorm. I almost went once and it was because of that once that I ended up at Stuart and Ruth's house.

I had made it through Torremolinos to the sounds of "OOOOOH, it's an English Ambulance" in every conceivable English accent, and was heading in Benidorm's direction. I fully intended on actually going, when two things changed my mind.

First, I stopped at a supermarket to do some shopping and was not exactly pleased to find that everyone around me spoke English with a northern accent. Even the Spanish. Whilst in the queue to pay a woman behind me tapped me on the shoulder and, when I turned around, asked "Are ya on ya 'ollydiz Chuck?"

"Umm, yeah."

"Eee, thas grand, 'ow many kiddies 'av ya got?"
"Sorry?" it was a question because it was actually another few minutes before I had worked out what she had said.
"Ah live 'ere ya know." And then the penny dropped. She had spotted someone she didn't recognize and needed to let the latest tourist know that she had moved out of the drabness of home and into the luxury of the sunshine life that most people only dream about. Sadly I wasn't in the least bit interested. I could hardly get out of the shop fast enough.
The second thing to happen was even worse.
It was a duel carriageway through what looked like a fairly new town that had been modeled on something from an old American movie. It also seemed to have traffic lights at about every one hundred yards and I kept finding them at red. Driving a British vehicle I was always sitting close to the pavement each time I stopped. It was late March and the sun was hot. I had the window down and the music up but even Freddie Mercury couldn't drown out the sound of the Liverpool accents on the pavement. It was then that I saw it. It was horrible!
About five feet five inches tall and about the same around the hips. And waist. And chest. It was clad in leggings and a tight fitting t-shirt. Bits of it were bobbing and wobbling all over the place as it moved along the pavement. There was a bit of a trend at the time for women to wear their hair tied in a loop right on top of their head. It looked good on some younger, slimmer girls, in the right circumstances, but not on creatures of this size and shape. It looked like an overweight Tellytubby. Then…

"Brrrraaaaanduuuuunnn!" it shouted at the top of its capacity and within three feet of my open window. "Gerrover 'ere ya little ****!" (I may be a bit old fashioned, but never in my life have I been able to say or even write that word, and I'm not about to start now.) I stared out of the window, horrified to discover that the creature was pushing a child's buggy. Not only that but it appeared to actually have a child under its control. Oh sweet mother of the gods - it was breeding! As the unfortunate offspring was being snatched off its feet and thrown into the buggy the lights changed and I got away as fast as I could. As soon as it was safe I moved over into the left hand lane and at the next set of lights I turned left and headed inland. And that is as close as I ever want to be to Benidorm.

I found a spot by a river to camp that night and when I looked at the map in the morning I realized that I wasn't that far from the village where Stuart and Ruth lived. So I had contacted Ruth and told her where I was. She had immediately insisted that I stop by and stay at their house for a few days. I had done so, to be informed that I was to stay for the usual two week holiday. At first I had agreed, but after little more than a week I had given up, made an excuse and left. Yes, I had known that Ruth was 'a little bossy', but I hadn't realized just how bad she could be. She had even tried to dictate what I ate and wore!
Now, here I was, heading for a full two weeks in that same house. I hoped I could cope. At the time I really believed that it would be better than spending those two weeks in that tiny Portuguese village where no one speaks English and where there was nothing to do other than walk by the river.

It took over two hours to get from the airport to the house, a trip that can be done in under an hour. Firstly, because Stuart took about three wrong turns and although he insisted that he did know how to get back onto the main road 'thank you very much miss Ruth the none driver' it was me who read the road signs and gave him directions as the two of them argued. And secondly because he drove so slowly I wondered if I should ask if there was anything wrong with the car. I thought that maybe we should get out and wind it up again or something. Ruth spent the entire time telling him where and when to turn and to look out for something on the other side of the road, and I wondered if she had changed her name to Hyacinth. But eventually I saw a sign for the village and quietly told Stuart to 'Try that way' and we finally made it to the house.

Ruth unlocked the door, carefully opened it and stepped inside. I followed and immediately tried to stop breathing too deeply.

"Still got the cats?" I said, not needing an answer.

"Of course," she said with a smile, completely missing my sarcasm.

I was not to stay upstairs in the room I had stayed in last time because there is no heating in the house and Ruth thought it would be too cold up there at that time of the year. So I had one of the Grandparents rooms downstairs. (For those who don't know; Although Spain can be hot during the day it can still get very cold at night).

When the house was built, between 400 to 600 years ago according to gossip, it was part of a huge manor house with the village around it possibly starting as mere hovels for the workers of the surrounding land. The main part of the house still stands and is for sale as a 17 bedroom home. It's been for sale for more than twenty years. Partly because it would take a monumental effort to make it even close to habitable, starting with adding electricity, a water supply and a sewer, rebuilding a few walls and employing someone with a bulldozer to find the front garden, and partly because no one wants seventeen bedrooms in a building that not only dominates a tiny village that's miles away from anywhere, but also sits almost opposite a convent.

The part of the house that is now the home of these two English friends of mine was once the offices and stables, and the main door was built big enough to bring the horses through; complete with cart loads of olives, grapes, tobacco, cotton or sugarcane or whatever else they grew. Or complete with the family carriage and high driver. Yes, those two front doors are enormous, and still there. And they still work. Although they are very rarely used and a smaller one has been cut into one of them, making entry much easier. I once mentioned to Stuart that if the weather got really bad he could bring his car inside and he told me that he would anyway, if he was allowed to, because the sun can do as much damage as any other weather.

You can still see the walkway in the floor of the living room, where the horses and carts would be taken through the building to the stables in the back, which also still exist. The ground has been tiled over but, with no real foundations, only part of the main room was done properly due to cost. The horse track was simply concreted over and is to be made into a feature at some point when enough money miraculously becomes available. On either side of these front doors is a bedroom. According to Ruth when this part of the building became a house, or maybe while it was still an office, whole families would live here, including the grandparents. These aged creatures would not be expected to be able to make the stairs so would have a bedroom on the ground floor, and the best place for that, for some reason unknown to me, was right by the front door. Personally I thought that if the building had once been offices, then that might be what these rooms were for, but I don't really know very much about Spanish history. So there I was to sleep. On the ground floor, right by the front door, in a room with 400 year old floor tiles that hadn't been level for 390 years.
I loved it.

The only thing I didn't like was the bars on the windows. I have a problem with being shut in; it's a form of claustrophobia. I always need to know that I can get out of anywhere. But I told myself that my room door was never locked and the main door to the house was right next to it with the key hanging in the lock. And those bars would allow me to have the window open during the night. Or rather the shutters.

The window was built into the thick wall with the sill about level with my chest. The window top was some six feet above this. There was no glass, just the bars and the two wooden shutters. Each shutter had its own window in it, with its own little shutter to close it off, and these did have a pane of glass each, but they were too high up to look out of. The shutters opened inwards, of course, and I could leave them open at any time and the bars would stop anyone getting in although everyone could look in. But I could open the shutters right up and drape a towel across the gap by pegging it to both catches, thereby allowing in plenty or air but preventing anyone from seeing anything.

Ruth is a bit of a kleptomaniac and a hoarder. She needs to own stuff, so the house, although huge, is packed with furniture, all of it looking as if it were meant to be there. There are four bedrooms in the main part of the house, the two downstairs and two up, with one of upstairs ones being two with a wall missing to make one large one. At the back of the house is another staircase leading to two more huge bedrooms, two roof terraces and a bathroom. It was one of these rooms that I had on my first visit, and every night I had to carry my aging dog up the stairs because they were too steep for him to climb. But he had loved sleeping outside on the terrace at night. He had loved the cool of the room during the daytime too, and the fact that none of the ten cats could get up there.
 As well as the two bedrooms the downstairs of the house consists of the enormous living room, a bathroom, a walled patio, a breakfast/dining room, kitchen, back room, stable and connecting store room, with a small garden at the back. Beyond the garden wall is the old Bodega and some more rooms of various size and shape that had once belonged to the manor house. But this is not part of my friends dwelling.

I absolutely love that house and the way it is furnished. The building has been added to and rearranged many times over the years and is now a wonderful muddle of rooms and stairs, terraces and patios. Ruth seems to have an eye for what furniture would go where with which sofa and what kind of lamp. If I were to describe it here it would sound like a jumble sale from the Victorian area, but to see it is to agree that it works.
It is fabulous.

CHAPTER TWO

That first morning I awoke quite late at about 9am. I really hate being in bed after that time, it feels like such a waste of a day to have it half over by the time I am washed and dressed. When I was washed and dressed I wandered into the kitchen and found the place empty of humans but with four furry creatures all sitting in a row and looking expectantly up at me. I wondered where the other cats were, there had been ten of them last time I was there. I didn't feed them; I didn't know what they ate or where it was. Two of them made a dive for the cat flap in the back door as soon as I moved and it was quite comical watching them both trying to get through it at the same time. The other two simply sat and scowled at me as I made coffee and breakfast.

As I did so I noticed something; the glass was still there. Or at least *a glass* because I doubted if it was the same one, on the draining board in the kitchen. A constant reminder of just what these two are really like.

Stuart has to take a lot of pills for one reason or another, and he keeps the glass out for that. He will open his pill bottles and packets and take the pills to the sink. He will fill the glass from the tap, use it to take his pills, tip the remaining water away and leave the glass out for the next time. The glass does not get washed up, ever. Stuart claims it isn't necessary because he will need it again, and Ruth refuses to wash it because she doesn't think it's her job to do so. The last time I had stayed, whenever I was washing up I would wash and dry it and put it back where I found it, but then I had been told not to do that.

In fact I had been given an order not to wash it! So there it sat, wet and collecting all sorts of germs and slowly getting more and more water stained until it would need to be thrown out. At that point Ruth would, no doubt, moan that he had ruined it. She certainly moaned at me, when I tried to wash it up, that he ruins all her glasses.

I thought that if she would just wash it up when she washed everything else, or if he would just leave it upside down to drain, the problem could be solved and several petty childish arguments could be avoided. But I had never said anything.

When I sat down in the breakfast/dining room – I already knew that it changed its name depending on Ruth's mood – I found a handsome but huge ginger tom sitting on the table, where he stayed, staring at me as I ate.
There was no sound anywhere in the house and the huge double doors to the walled patio were still closed, as were the two huge doors from the back room to the garden. Clearly I was the only one out of bed.
I sat in silence for a while and checked Facebook and I became aware of a metallic clicking sound. The table I was sitting at was an old school table and still had the brass ink well covers. The ginger tom was playing with one of these covers, flicking the lid back and forth, opening the hole and putting his paw into it before seeming to get annoyed and sliding the lid closed again. I waited until he opened it again and leaned over to poke my fingers up through the hole from the underside. The cat reared up on his hind end and dived forward with both front paws to grab at my fingers which I, of course, withdrew. Grabbing onto thin air the cat lost his balance and skidded off the table onto the chair beside me. But the seat cover on that wasn't attached so he slid off that too and hit the floor. A ginger line seemed to appear from under the chair to the kitchen as he fled as fast as he could. My first encounter with Thomas had not been good. But he soon forgave me and before long we became good friends.

Ruth appeared just before 11 am, made herself a coffee and sat next to me at the table. We chatted for a while and my legs started to fidget due to lack of movement. I wanted to be up and doing something. Eventually I said that I would go to the village shop to get something for my lunch as I didn't expect them to feed me for two weeks, and I managed to escape. I got back, made my lunch, sat and ate it and even made another coffee and still Ruth sat there in her nightdress and dressing gown. Stuart was pottering about in the garden but Ruth seemed content not to move. She didn't get dressed until 3 o'clock in the afternoon and it wasn't even Sunday!

During that time she told me that six of their cats had died and she wasn't having any more because at 58 she was too old to cope with too many. "I'm 69 and I cope" was Stuart's only contribution to the conversation. The four remaining cats were named Thomas, Gail, Maggie and Linda, because Ruth liked 'real names and not stupid ones'.

Gail was the skitty one who had escaped from the house next door – the opposite side to the old Manor house - the previous year, which told me that seven of the others had died in the past two years, not just six. Since living here these two had had anything up to 30 cats at any one time and now they were down to four. No wonder their garden was blooming, it must have been well fertilized! Poor Gail had been left alone, shut in the walled concrete yard of the house next door with several bowls of water and a huge tube of dry cat food, for several months. Apparently the idea was that a cat would keep the rats away as the family spent time at their other home in Barcelona. I admit that this confused me. Surely if the yard was unoccupied and closed up and locked there would be no food around to encourage the rats in. But if there was cat food in the yard…..well…rats eat cat food. I know my son was told not to feed it to his pet rats because it would make them fat, but I doubted if wild rats would be so health conscious. It would be like expecting a hungry five year old to turn down a Happy Meal on the off chance there might be a salad around.

Eventually this poor cat had found a way onto the roof where she could look down into the garden and patio of this house. She had then walked from the roof along the top of a crumbling wall and jumped eight feet down onto a barbed wire topped wall and then another six feet into the garden. I have serious suspicions that Stuart and his ladder may have had something to do with this great escape. But once in this garden it is impossible for any animal to get back out again so Gail had been named and kept. And Gail was currently in season.

Imagine an angry two year old child screaming the word NO with as much effort as can be mustered. That is the sound that this tiny creature forced out of her mouth to bounce off the walls and reverberate around the house in her desperate search for a mate.

Thomas, the ginger tom who had been fixed, was big and beautiful, loving and playful and, best of all, quiet. Maggie was old, had a problem with her eyes and was possibly deaf. Her mother Linda was said to be unsociable but spent a lot of time sitting on my lap and trying to steal the food from my plate. All were rescue cats and Ruth gave out the impression that it was she who did the rescuing and caring, but I later realized that this was not the case. Stuart was the big cat lover.

Those first few days were spent in the house. I went to the local shop to buy food, even though Stuart had driven to the next village to buy me some rice cakes because he had remembered that I cannot eat bread, and I wandered around the village a bit. But that was all we did. Stuart pottered about wiping table tops in the garden or patio or fiddling with plants, and Ruth sat about for most of the day. They both spent a lot of time puffing on their vape things because they had given up smoking and Ruth told me how stupid I had been to drive around Europe in a van that was obviously ready to break down. I must have known it was going to break down and should never have left. Of course I should have known it was 'in that state'. *They* would never have done that, *they* would have bought a new van and made sure it wasn't going to break down. Stuart and I sat quietly not even mentioning the time they drove to Benidorm but had to get a taxi back because the head gasket on their car had blown, as Ruth, who has never even sat in a driver's seat let alone actually driven a car, explained how much more she knew about vehicles than the two ex lorry drivers, both with a PCV license, sitting in the same room. In fact, Stuart is also an ex London bus driver (I just drove a Land Train) and I believe he drove and looked after bigger vehicles than that during his time in the army. Yet he kept quiet and only stared out of the window into the corner of the patio as I took this education class in mechanical knowledge from a woman who had once asked me why I thought I needed a battery for my engine. That was how this man had managed to cope with her for thirty eight years. He basically ignored her. Stuart is the type of man who needs a bossy woman to tell him how to live his life, some men just do. But even he has his limits.

I began to count the days until my return to Portugal and wondered if it would be possible to change to an earlier flight. By the third day I knew I had made a mistake in being there. Age and confinement had made Ruth way worse than I had ever imagined possible.

Ruth gleefully told me that it was not often she had to leave the house and I soon realized that even her daily trips to the communal bin at the end of the street were avoided if she could force Stuart to go. She flat refused to take the recycling because that was 'His job' and if she didn't make him do it he would sit about all day 'doing fuck all'. I wondered if she believed it was fairies who did all the painting and decorating in the place, who cut the lawn and tended the garden. Maybe she believed the plants watered themselves and the patio was self cleaning. I said nothing, but I did start taking the recycling out myself saying that I needed something to do. The recycling bins were two streets away and it was lovely to be out of the house. I would drop that off and then meander around the village which usually took at least ten minutes; it's not a big village. Thankfully Ruth didn't know that the recycling bins had been moved closer to their house some two years previously and she still believed they were several streets away so she didn't think too much of it if I took my time. Apparently I was still 'A lot quicker than him'. As she didn't know where the bins were she didn't know about the coffee shop across the road. Stuart clearly wasn't as dumb as she thought. But why she never wanted to leave the house was a total mystery to me.

I once suggested she join me for a wander around the village or a walk by the river but she just looked at me in horror. "What on earth for?" she demanded. "Walking just for the sake of it is a stupid waste of time," she told me, while she sat in her dressing gown flicking though Amazon for stuff she didn't need.

The only outing that first week was when we went to a nearby town to go shopping. I had not been able to change my flight without extra cost so I had decided that I would cope a second week; and things really weren't so bad. Or so I thought.

When Ruth announced one morning that we were going to the nearest town to do some 'proper' shopping I wondered if she meant food, or were we going to wander around the shops looking at stuff I didn't want and she didn't need. We had spent a bit of time doing that the last time I had stayed, but thankfully this was now a redundant pastime.
"Oh, where are we going?" I asked.
"Well, there isn't a Lidl so we'll have to go to Mercadona," she said. OK, we were only going food shopping, so I couldn't help but wonder why she had got dressed up and even put makeup on. Gone was the nightdress and dressing gown, and gone were the torn t-shirt and tatty leggings with holes in that she used when she did finally get dressed, and in their place was a smart pair of jeans and a very nice top. On her feet, instead of the worn down cheap flip flops, she had a pretty pair of shoes with some kind of butterfly on the toes. It looked as if she might even have put a decent bra on! We were to leave at precisely that minute so I grabbed a cardie and my backpack and felt grateful that I always keep a rolled up shopping bag in it together with my purse. But I wasn't to use my own shopping bag, apparently that 'wasn't right' so I was to use one that Ruth gave me. By then I knew better than to disagree.
And so we drove the several miles to Xativa.

On the way there I was told which shops were the best for food shopping and what sort of things I could buy as if I had never been to Spain, or even a supermarket, before. And they both talked about how they wished there was a Lidl in Xativa because this was defiantly the shop they liked best. Stuart was still talking about Lidl and its prices as we got out of the car and he said again, "I really wish they would build one here."
"You mean like that one over there?" I asked, pointing to the Lidl store across the road.

They both turned to stare at it; they had no idea that it was there. But, in all fairness, we did learn later that it had only been there for about three months.

We visited two shops in this town, Mercadona and the pet shop. After all the praise they had given to the other supermarket they didn't want to go there. I think this was because it was across the road and that would be too far for them to walk. They don't walk very far at all. Stuart will park as close to the shop door as he can. Even waiting, if he has seen the relevant movement, for the closest space to become available. Ruth will moan about how everyone parks too close to the shop if there isn't a vacant space close to the shop for them to use. Stuart does not help with the shopping at all. He follows Ruth around the shop and does absolutely nothing. He would probably get told off if he attempted to put anything in the basket so he just wanders aimlessly behind her. He doesn't help carry the bags either, nor put them into the car boot. He has a bad back, or a sore arm, or something wrong with some part of him that no one knows about and he just can't carry heavy bags without passing out. Or so he told me. But he does pay for everything.

We drove from the supermarket to the pet shop because it was too far to walk at about 100 yards and while we were still outside it I looked around and noticed a large hill with a castle on the top. It looked interesting. "Have you ever been up there?" I asked.

"Yes, once, a long time ago," Stuart said.

"Nothing worth seeing up there," Ruth said.

"I'd like to go up and have a look," I said.

"Huh, you'll be going on your own then," spat Ruth, "It's a long bloody way up there and there's nothing to see when you get there, just some old bricks. Anyway, you'd never make it to the top in this heat, you're too old now."

It was early March and not that hot, and I didn't consider myself to be too old for anything except running, and that was only since I had needed operations on both feet. I made up my mind there and then to visit the castle as soon as possible.

I bought some coffee on that shopping trip and I put it on the tray in the kitchen. I had been using their coffee since I had been there and had decided it was time I paid for a jar. I assumed we would all just use it. But I was wrong. My coffee was crap and she wasn't going to even bother to try it. She didn't need to try it, she knew it was crap. I could use it if her's wasn't good enough for me, but she wasn't going to touch that shit. The English one that Ruth insists on is very expensive and the Spanish one I had bought looked and – to me at least – tasted exactly the same but was less than half the price. I continued to buy and use it myself. And I rinsed my cup out after I had used it.
You see, we were only to use one cup each all day. That cup should not be washed up each time as it's a waste of water, but should be just left on the tray with the tea and coffee jars to wait for the next use. I just about coped with this and kept quiet because I had already been told off over coffee and didn't want to make things worse.
The thing is this; - In my home, if someone else is there and I make a coffee or a cup of tea I will offer one to whoever is there as well. I think most people do this. But in this house that's not the way it works. In this house you only make your own coffee or tea and you ignore anyone else. Guest or not. I did make Ruth a coffee once and was told it was vile and not to do it again. I assume that Stuart had learned this lesson many years ago. I was told not to offer to make him anything because he is lazy and should learn to do it himself. Which is exactly what he has been doing for the past 38 years.
I also got into trouble over the kettle.

I think modern kettles are strange things. At home I use a glass one that sits on a gas hob and gets washed up with the dishes every day. I don't fill the kettle from the tap; I fill the mug and pour that into the kettle, thereby only heating exactly what I need. If I want tea I let it boil, if I want instant coffee I turn off the gas when I think it's hot enough. I'm actually quite capable of doing that without the kettle flashing any lights at me and without the need for an App on my phone. My kettle is never left sitting with water inside but it still gets dull after a time so, now and then, I will boil a cup of water with lemon juice to make it shiny again. I have never felt the need to pay £60 for a kettle that tells me when the water is at a certain temperature to save me money while needing to have a range of lights constantly on to show me the power is getting to its relevant parts. And people leave these plugged in! Really, do you need a reminder that power is getting to the kettle while on your midnight trip to the fridge? And many people let them get so scaled up that it's probably costing them three times as much to use anyway.
Ruth's kettle wasn't one of the ones with flashing lights, but it did have so much scale that the lid wouldn't close properly, thereby often causing it to continue to boil away quite happily, steaming up the kitchen until someone came along and turned it off.
As soon as I had found myself alone in the kitchen I had emptied it of its water and chipped away at the scale around the lid with a knife. I got enough off to close the lid but I couldn't get at the filter that covers the spout. That was securely scaled to its morning and had no intention of moving. After giving it a good rinse I realized that it had been a fairly decent kettle at some point because the heating element was just the flat bottom so it allowed people like me to only heat exactly what they need. I added a mug full of water and made my coffee.

Ruth had appeared just as I was sitting down. She had gone to the kettle and noticed that it I had left the lid up. Just as I had planned she looked inside. "There's no water in the kettle!" she announced as if it were the strangest thing in the world. Which was why I had left the lid up, so no one simply turned it on while it was empty.
"I used it." I said.
"Well fill it up again then."
"OK, sorry."
I was then given a lecture on how to treat a kettle.
It must be emptied every morning because yesterday's water will have gone off, (I didn't ask how). The kettle must be left with water in it at all times or Stuart would turn it on and set fire to it and 'burn the fucking house down'. And I must fill the kettle to the top each time I used it or it wouldn't work properly. I didn't ask about that either, I just nodded and said, "OK" as I was told that I really should have known how to look after a kettle seeing as I claim to have done some sort of café management thing.
It was an HND in Hotel and Catering management actually but I decided it would be best if I didn't mention that.

That night I sipped hot lemon water out of a clean cup and looked at my map. I found that the railway line running behind the village eventually ends up in Xativa. And that the village even had a station. I found the relevant website and then the train time table and the following day I went for a day out. I did suggest that Stuart and Ruth join me and was extremely grateful when they declined. Ruth reminded me that I am old and it's hot and I wouldn't make it all the way up the hill to the castle anyway. She suggested I take the train.
"There's a train goes up there?" I asked.
"Yes, one of those kiddie tourist things like you drive."
"I drive a Land Train."
"Yes, a kiddie thing."

I decided not to bother, she would never understand. I also decided not to ride the train. I had once had to do a hill start while driving the Exmouth Land Train up Carlton Hill with 60 adult passengers onboard and a stream of traffic behind me. I know how scary that was so I didn't fancy being a passenger on one that was going up a much steeper hill. Ruth was still talking, telling me that I wouldn't have much time because I would need to get the 3 o'clock train back so my whole day was going to be spent sitting on a train and wasting time and money.

I pointed out that there was a 6 o'clock train but that suggestion was ignored. I did not make things worse by saying it was possible to get out of bed and go out before midday.

The following morning, before the other two had even thought about waking up, I walked to where my map said the station was and found a raised bit of concrete with what appeared to be a rundown East End bus shelter on it. The walls were covered in graffiti, it stank of urine, the paint was peeling from the metal and all the glass had been swept into a pile and pushed across the concrete to be left in one of those square holes in the pavement that trees grow out of. There was no tree in this hole and it looked as if there had never been. I looked along the pavement and saw that none of the square holes had anything growing in them and the pavement ended abruptly about 25 yards either side of where I stood. The neat and tidy, unused road came out of the village on one side of me and ended with the end of the pavement on the other side. I guessed that the plans for a station and maybe some nice new houses had once been made. I suspected that the road was to eventually go to a nearby town or maybe meet up with the duel carriageway that could currently only be accessed from a small road on the other side of the village. The problem was that shortly after the work had started the Great Spanish Recession had hit when the banks admitted they didn't have the money for anyone to pay for all this after all. Sights like this are all too common in Spain at the moment and I have never been sure if it should be classed as a good thing for the environment, or a bad thing for the people.

After the village, with its five streets and four shops that were clearly once just someone's front room, Xativa seemed like a major metropolis, but in reality it's probably less than a quarter of the size of Norwich. I read that it had a population of around 30,000 but that it is a fairly big and popular shopping centre for the people of the smaller towns and villages in the area. It's a nice place and I found some rather interesting streets and some rather interesting buildings, many of which are sadly falling apart. Some of the streets appeared to be made of marble. Maybe they are, maybe they just look like it, I don't really know, but I wouldn't want to be there in the rain just in case. I imagine they would get very slippery.

I wandered around the town for a bit and then headed up the hill to the castle.

It looked to me like one hill with two peeks and the castle straddles both peeks. It reminded me, a little, of the Towers of San Marino.

I saw a road and the beginnings of a foot path. Reading the signs on the way I learned that the path was mainly the original route to the castle. So I followed that and although I didn't exactly run up it, I didn't feel old at all. Half the path is now missing, but it's possible to follow the tracks as millions of people have done before. I found all sorts of plants and caves and interesting stones and places to look out over the town below and I even spotted a huge and strange looking cat sitting in the shade watching the world go by. It looked a bit like a cross between a Main Coon and a cheater. Whatever it was, it was in no mood to move and simply stared at me as I walked passed. Thankfully.

When I got to the top I found the train Ruth had been talking about.

Flipping cheek! I do not drive a tractor with two dirty boxes on the back; I drive a real Land Train, with three proper carriages that are kept spotlessly clean. I was quite insulted!

I spent a long time up in that castle. Although it's now little more than a ruin I still found it fascinating. I learned that Hannibal had once lived there and that his son was born there, although there was no mention of the elephants. To be honest, not much of that original castle still exists. They may claim it has always been the Xativa Castle, but the building itself has been rebuilt many times. I think the earliest of what is left now could be Islamic. It was a little difficult to understand the writing on the posts because it wasn't the best of translations, but the basics were there.

I managed to work out that around 1412 the place had housed its own prison and some famous bloke was impression there for years in a tiny room with no windows and therefore no light. When he was finally released he stepped out into the bright sunshine of the middle of the day and was immediately blinded by the light. He died later that same day.

In 1522 the Santa Fe Tower was completely destroyed when it was struck by lightning. That might not have been so bad in itself, but the tower just happened to be where they stored the gunpowder.

Almost 200 years later the place was again rebuilt after some war or other, and fifty years after that it was shattered during two earth quakes.

I also read that in 1870 a restaurant was built and opened to the public, but I couldn't work out by whom. Nor why anyone would want to walk all the way up there just to eat.

There was a lot to explore and I was enthralled by the view of the land around it. You literally can see for miles. I had my picnic up there and got chatting to some kids from a local school. They were meant to be on a history trip but seemed to prefer to practice their English. One child told me that the cannons were from the 1500's and explained to me, in great detail, how they worked and the damage they could do. Another child told me how much fun they were to climb on and slid off. I learned all about the bad teacher with the smelly breath and the good teacher who let them climb on the cannons; and how I should go to Gandia because it is so beautiful there. (It is; I have been several times.) One of them also told me to be careful because I might not be able to get home. I didn't know what he meant at the time and there wasn't time to ask because the teacher called and they had to go. But I found out later that night.

I got back to the house quite late and Ruth was in a good mood for a change and even asked about my day. I didn't tell her much about it because it was clear she wasn't actually interested, but at least she was trying to be polite. I did tell her about the kids I had met and that one of them had suggested I go to Gandia and I mentioned that I hadn't been for some time and I knew she like the town so maybe……
But she was talking over me telling me how she didn't believe any Spanish kid would stop to talk to me and they certainly wouldn't speak English that well.
I left her in the main room and went to make myself something to eat. When I got back she said "I thought we would go to Gandia for the day tomorrow, if you like. Stuart needs to get out and walk a bit, he needs the exercise." He looked up from where he was eating his dinner in front of the TV, but he said nothing. "Unless you want to go to Benidorm," she joked. I didn't know whether to laugh or throttle her.

I forced a laugh, "Gandia sounds good," I said, and it was arraigned.
But we never got there.

This was Friday 13th March 2020.

CHAPTER THREE

I don't follow the news. I don't read the papers and I don't often watch TV. It's always too depressing. The last time I bought a newspaper it was because I was in it, and I had read half the story before I realized it was meant to be mine. They had completely disregarded anything I had said and made up something totally different. They had even stated that I had done one thing in June and another thing six month later in September. I had called and asked how they managed to fit six months into the time between June and September and had been told that details like that didn't matter. I have not paid attention to anything in the media since then. And I took the attitude I have now. If it doesn't directly affect me, I don't want to know.

Selfish?

Possibly, but a lot less stressful.

Since I had been at this house we had watched a couple of movies but I had paid no attention to the news. It was in Spanish anyway and Stuart was the only one of us who was able to understand it.

I do have Facebook and so I was aware of this virus called Covid-19 that was sweeping across the world and causing people to stock pile toilet paper and argue over pasta, but I didn't know enough about it to take it seriously. I admit that I had taken to checking Google news for the odd article on it but, not trusting any media, had not taken it too much notice. I was aware that people were being asked to be careful, to social distance where possible, to wash their hands more and to try and stay healthy, and I was aware that the hand sanitizer I had wanted to buy was out of stock everywhere or had quadrupled in price. I also knew that a few people had died. But I was not aware of what things were really like.

We three were sitting by the log fire in front of the TV. Stuart was watching the Spanish news and Ruth, with headphones on, was watching something in her ibook/notepad thing. I also had my headphones on and was watching a history documentary on YouTube on my phone. A young Richard 2nd was dealing with the Peasants' Revolt when Stuart swore loudly and sat bolt upright in his seat. He had received a text message from the local council.
"What the Fuck's wrong with you?" snapped Ruth, all her good mood having been used up.
"We're not going to Gandia tomorrow," he said.
"Yes we fucking are, what are you on about?"
"We're not" he said. "We're not going anywhere. We're not allowed to go anywhere. Not now."
He then explained what his message had said. The country was going into a state of emergency at midnight, just one hour away. From that point on we would be in Lockdown and would not be allowed out of the house except to go food shopping. Everything was to stop. There were to be no busses, no schools, no factories unless they produced essential items, no shops other than pharmacies and food shops, no movement at all.
He looked at me and said, "Your flight will be cancelled. You'll be staying here for a couple more weeks."
To say that my heart sank would be a huge understatement. I felt it plummet from my chest through my abdomen and thump into my nether region like a blue whale falling from the sky. As it slithered towards my feet Stuart changed the channel on the TV and told us what was going on in the news. He translated quite well. They were saying the same thing. This virus was way worse than we had thought and we were having to do this Lockdown to help save lives. The idea being that, not only should we not get close enough to anyone else to spread the germs, but by staying home we would cause fewer accidents and therefore free up the hospitals to allow them to deal with those suffering and dying from Covid.

Once it had all sunk in Ruth and I looked at each other and shrugged. "Looks like you're staying on." She said.

The following day I learned via Google that Portugal was not in a state of emergency and the border was still open. I tried to bring my flight forward to as soon as possible but while I was doing that I got a text message from the airline saying that it had been cancelled. I looked at trains; cancelled. I looked at busses; cancelled. I thought about hitch hiking, but I didn't think it would work as well as the last time I had hitched from Portugal to Italy in the 1980's.
I confess I even thought about walking, but we weren't allowed outside so spending two or three weeks walking across Spain was possibly a silly idea. Looking back now, I wish I had done it.
I was stuck.

Stuart and Ruth were ok about it and Ruth started making plans about when we would go shopping and how we would all just have to get on with each other. I felt they were actually being really good about having to have me stay there. She cleared a shelf in the fridge and told me it was for me to use and brought down some sheets from upstairs that I should put on my bed. I was to keep the others in my room, once they had been washed, for the following week. She also brought down a nightdress and dressing gown that I was to start using because she didn't think the t-shirt I had been sleeping in was suitable. It had been suitable for the past ten years and no one ever saw it except on the washing line so I didn't understand why I should now disregard it. But I did as I was told. She was being helpful, but it felt as if she had suddenly become my mother as she reeled off a list of house rules like how I was to have my shower in the morning while the water heater was on (and not in the evening after the solar panel had had the chance to heat the water for free). And how I was not to wash up during the day as it was a waste of water, but everything had to be kept for one 'wash up' at the end of the day. I was soon to learn that the rules of washing up were to change on a fairly regular basis, and I wasn't to be told about them until after I had done the wrong thing.

Stuart kept reading out bits of news and said that we were not allowed to even leave the house, and could only go to the supermarket or the pharmacy. The local council would be providing facemasks "Not for you, because you don't live here" he told me, until people could buy their own, and no one was to get within two meters of anyone they didn't live with. Stuart made a few funny comments about how he should stay two meters away from Ruth, just to be sure, but I was the only one who laughed.

When the masks were delivered Ruth went to the empty house next door and took the two that had been posted into their letter box so that I could have one. No one was in the house as they were still in Barcelona and Ruth had the key because she was meant to be dropping in once a week to make sure the cats had water.
Yes, it had happened again.

The neighbor, aware that Gail had escaped but not where to, had acquired two kittens – brother and sister – and had left them there alone, just as they had done with Gail.
We talked about those cats now as we realized that the family would not be coming back for the foreseeable future. Ruth and I ended up going to the house to check on them.
The house next door was cold and felt damp and the garden turned out to be a concrete jungle of half built rooms behind the house. Each room appeared to be filled with some sort of building material or the kind of crap people keep but don't want in their house. Two cats had been left here alone for several weeks and they could not get out. To say the place stank was an understatement.
The water bowls were empty but covered with scale and the food tube was moldy. We cleaned the tube and washed the bowls before filling them up. We did not see the cats. Ruth told me that they would probably be about six months old by then.
"And they are brother and sister?" I asked.
"Yes,"
"So how long do you expect to only find two of them in here?"
"That's the problem," she said, "But there's nothing we can do about it; we'll just have to keep an eye on them." She picked up a shovel that had been leaning against a wheelbarrow and scooped up enough cat poo to create a path across the yard, there wasn't even anywhere for them to bury it, and then we left.

I got an email from Raymond telling me that he had stripped my engine and found a problem with the clutch as well. I had been half expecting that as the foot peddle had been sticky for some time. I had mentioned it to the mechanic in Cornwall and he had told me "Um, yeah, well, it's OK for now; I'll have a look at it when you get back." He had assured me that it wouldn't be a problem for a while yet. But Raymond now had the engine apart so now seemed like a good time to fix it. Raymond explained the problem and sent me a photograph. I had absolutely no idea what I was looking at but a quick Google search told me I needed a new clutch. In fact, comparing the photographs online with the one Raymond had sent told me I probably needed a new clutch about six months earlier. Not only is Raymond the best, he is also the cheapest so I told him to go ahead and do it. After all, I had plenty of time.

The next email I had from him was to say that Portugal had now gone into Lockdown and he couldn't go to work. He said that he would try and sneak in so the van would be ready when I got back, even thought the border was now closed, but I told him not to. I really didn't think it would be more than a couple of weeks and Portugal was very strict on its Lockdown rules. Raymond worked mostly on cars; I think my van is the biggest thing he has ever had in his garage. Because he did not work on Lorries or emergency vehicles he was forced to close and stay home.

Now I really started to feel trapped.

That van is my lifeline. My way of being free as well as getting to work when I'm home. Now it was in a different country, locked inside a building, and without an engine. While I was trapped here.

I tried to contact the British embassy for advice but I guess every other Brit was thinking the same thing because it was a couple of weeks before I got a response to say that someone will get back to me when they can.

I had only brought two weeks' worth of my medication so a visit to the pharmacy was called for. Stuart told me that all pharmacists in Spain had to speak English and the ones in the village were very good. At home I could have got what I needed on prescription, but had found it cheaper in the local health food shop, and my GP had said it was just the same so I had been buying it. I was pleased to find I could do the same in Spain, even if I did have to explain that acidophilus is not, in fact, folic acid.

So I donned a mask and set off. It was only two streets away and I expected to be back quite soon. But social distancing had now become a thing.

The pharmacy was only letting one person at a time inside the shop so everyone was asked to wait at a distance outside. And they did as they were asked and duly waited across the road. In a group!

I went to that side of the road and took up my place, two meters away from the group. The group saw me and shuffled further away, together. This was a very small village in the heart of Valencia, miles away from any tourist area, and I wasn't local. I wondered what the Spanish words were for 'I don't have leprosy.'

A week later we heard that the UK had also gone into Lockdown. But there it was slightly different. Shops and schools were shut and people were asked to stay home. Panic buying was in full swing and toilet roll and pasta couldn't be found for love nor money. My friend pointed out on Facebook that he will continue to work as his job was essential, and indeed he did work 'on the front line' as he put it for the next few months. I never did manage to work out why delivering cakes was considered essential, but I guess it came under the heading of 'Food'. I had no idea the DIY shops were considered essential either; nor why, when asked to stay home, everyone was out walking and posting photos of the great new places they had discovered and the new people they had met. And I really never understood why, when asked to social distance to try and stop the spread of a virus that could kill, people thought it necessary to meet up in groups of thousands and roam the streets shouting about how much better they could run the country than the present government. I never understood why everyone blamed the government anyway; it's not as if they knew what to do any better than anyone else. Only one thing was certain, if the shops were closing then at least the DFS sale must finally be over.

After a couple of weeks things were still OK in the house. Ruth was still her bossy self, but she was trying to be nice. The fact that she feels she is always right about everything and literally cannot be wrong was beginning to get on my nerves a bit, and I did a lot of lip biting to keep quiet. I took to getting up early as they stayed in bed until around 11am and by that time I tried to be outside. Not able to sit still for long I started walking outside the house. This was not strictly legal at the time, but the police had seen me, watched me long enough to realize what I was doing, and left me alone. By my reckoning it was about 50 yards from the front door to the corner of the street passing the seventeen bed-roomed house next door. So I downloaded a book from my local library at home and put on my earphones. I then went outside and walked. I walked to the end of the street and back to the door again, and again, and again. I did this for about an hour every day. I saw no one, except for those two police in the car and the odd dog walker on their way to the park.

In the afternoon I would disappear into my room to write or read or watch YouTube. Stuart would also spend the afternoons in his room and this became a sort of 'give each other space' time. Ruth would sit in the breakfast/dining room with her laptop or potter about doing housework. I was not allowed to help with the housework because she wanted it done properly.

She taught me how to use the washing machine.

I like washing machines in launderettes. I like them because they are simple and I don't have to pay for them, or even think about them when they go wrong. And when they do go wrong there is always one right next to it that I can use. I don't have to clean them or insure them, or treat them with anything to stop them scaling up. And if I haven't got the money to pay for a wash, I wait until I have, I don't build up any bill that I later can't afford to pay. Most of them have three settings; Hot, Warm or Cold, and that is good enough. There really isn't any point in complicating anything. In Some countries I don't even have to buy washing liquid because the launderettes provide that as well.
Now I had to use a domestic machine with a control panel that seemed to have come from the cockpit of a 747, so I asked Ruth to explain it to me.
Realizing that the cycle she was explaining I should use would take about an hour and a half I asked if there was a shorter one.
"Does it matter?" she said.
"Well, no not really, it just seems like a waste of power and water to have that many washes and rinses."
"It's the only cycle that works," she said.
I was quiet, so she went onto explain to me that the machine has never worked properly since they first had it plumbed in.
"If it didn't work from new couldn't you get your money back or get them to give you one that worked properly?" I asked.
"No, the company went bust, they don't exist anymore."
"I mean from the day you realized it didn't work."
"That was the day it was fitted," she said, "And the day they went bust and disappeared."
She left the room, a Ruth way of saying that the conversation was over, mainly because she couldn't think of any more excuses. Stuart, who had been watching this while pretending to sort out his several shelves of medications looked sadly at me and quietly said, "The instructions are in Spanish and she won't admit she can't read them."

He told me that as long as I only pushed the 'On' button to start it and didn't touch anything else I wouldn't get told off.

I tried to keep in touch with friends in Portugal. Not just too see how they were and because they are friends, but to keep abreast of what was really going on. And a lot was going on. Foreigners who had lived in Portugal, quietly and with no permanent residence, for several years were being found and sent home. Several of them had no home to go to but still had to leave Portugal. Many campervans, motorhomes and caravans were queuing up to leave while others were trying to hide in the hope of attempting to stay. Most of these were being found and moved on. One family claimed it was unfair because they had come from Brazil five years previously and had jobs while their kids were in school. They had continued to live in their caravan without becoming residents due to cost, now they were told they had to leave Portugal. I never found out what happened to them but, quite frankly, if you break the countries rules for five years you need to be deported when you get found out.

One English campsite owner was found to have at least eight English caravans or campervans on his site that had all been there for several years, paying cash that he did not declare. They got sent out of the country while he got arrested. People were complaining and explaining that they didn't have homes to go to in their own countries anymore and Portugal was explaining that it didn't care. If you didn't have residency in Portugal you left, simple. I found I agreed with Portugal, I felt they were putting their own people first, just as they should. I became very grateful to be where I was because had I stayed in my van in the garage in Portugal I would have had major problems. I would have needed to hide. Not being a resident I couldn't stay, but not having an engine meant it would have been hard to leave. The van being my home meant I had nowhere to go to anywhere else.

Crikey! What would I have done?

With plans to travel to Vietnam the following year (Flying, not driving) I was keeping an eye on things there too. They were well ahead of the rest of the world and had already closed their borders and shut down their schools. Areas were being sealed off for two or three weeks at a time and even people returning home to the country were forced to quarantine in government provided, very basic conditions.

The stories from Madrid were that the death toll was rising and they were running out of places to keep the bodies and there were rumors of freezer lorries sitting in hospital grounds. An Englishman was arrested for being on the street without good reason and, believing he could abuse the Spanish police just as he would the English, he had resisted arrest. Somehow he had fallen and hurt his face and would be certainly going to jail just as soon as he got out of hospital. An English tourist had decided she was above the law and dived into a closed off swimming pool at a holiday resort and didn't understand why the police dragged her out and arrested her. I wondered if the jail cell was warm because I had seen no sign of even a towel on the news report, but then I found I didn't really care because she should have stayed out of the pool. And right around the globe people were sitting in airports insisting that extra planes be acquired from somewhere so they could get home while demanding compensation for the loss of their holiday. While the streets of London thronged with people and the underground was reported to be packed, and while the streets of Italy echoed with the sound of people singing on their balconies, this tiny village echoed with the sound of silence until the daily information announcement, a relic from the days of Franco, blasted along the tiny, house lined streets at full volume.

I was told that back in the days of Franco all newspapers were banned in Spain. I honestly have no idea if this is true, but I had learned not to question Ruth by this point. She told me that no one was allowed to know much about what was really going on and so to keep the population informed, and controlled, speakers were set up along streets and news announcements were made daily.

In some small villages these speakers are still used for local information, like letting people know that someone in the village has died or telling them it's time to move their car to park on the other side of the street, or to remind them that it is their turn to clean the street. Ignoring those who worked nights and wanted to sleep during the day, and regardless of the mothers who had just got their toddler down for a nap, these speakers would shriek out music at top volume to attract people's attention at least twice a day. When the music finished an announcement would be made at a volume designed to reach those working in the surrounding fields. The fact that those surrounding fields had long since been turned into a half used industrial estate and covered with mostly empty factories didn't seem to mean the volume should be turned down. For the first three weeks of my stay I honestly believed that the speaker for our village was right outside my window, but on further investigation it was discovered to be about 200 meters away on another street. I was grateful to be in such an old house because it is difficult to rattle the walls when they are two feet thick. I felt so sorry for the people living in the newer buildings closer to the church where the speaker was. I also felt it was good that the cemetery was nowhere near the church because even the dead wouldn't be able to sleep through one of the announcements.

But I got used to them and sometimes Stuart would tell me what they said. This usually resulted in an argument between him and Ruth as she told him he was wrong and needed to wash his ears, or to learn to listen properly. Once this situation resulted in an argument about how to do a post mortem and how they would both like to bury each other under the stable floor.
The only thing that really annoyed me about these twice daily intrusions into the absolute silence was the music they had decided would be good to play first. Why was it always a Spanish version of Gloria Gayonr's 'I Will Survive?'

****

With little to do I started glancing at the news and spending longer on Facebook and I read was that there was no Coronavirus; that it was all the fault of 5G masts.
 I read more.
Apparently 5G masts were being installed in England and this was causing people to die of radiation poisoning. Confused, I did some research and leaned that 5G had been around in Europe and parts of the US for some time, yet it was only just now being introduced into the UK. For some unknown reason people were claiming that the deaths attributed to Covid-19 were really due to radiation from these masts and the virus was some sort of government cover up. I spent a half hour reading 'reports' on the internet, learning how people were tearing down mobile phone masts and then going home to use the internet to complain to their phone provider that they couldn't get a signal. Apparently this was all done to uncover some sort of government conspiracy about radiation poisoning which was somehow designed to control people by killing them off. Then I turned to Facebook to see what sort of drivel some of the morons on there were writing.
Oh it was such fun; it really brightened my day.

I found one thread where several people claimed they 'knew for sure' that there was no virus and 5G was to blame. They claimed to have 'friends' who worked in certain places. They claimed not to have been brainwashed into believing anything other than the 'truth' and they honestly expected people to believe them. The more I read the more I imagined people sitting at their computers wearing tinfoil covered colanders on their heads, after struggling out of their special jackets and murdering a couple of nurses.
On one thread I posted a link to an article about how 5G had been in Europe for several months and asked why people were not dying then, but only now. There were three different responses.
1) The article was lies.
2) People were dying back then but the government covered it up.
3) The problem lays dormant and doesn't show itself for several months.

Naming each poster I asked three more questions.
1) Could they show me the proof of the lies?
2) Which government did the covering up? Because this involved several different countries.
3) If the problem doesn't show itself for several months why are people dying so soon in the UK?

The responses took a while for me to read due to the poor spelling, bad grammar and the use of some sort of language that was possibly a throwback to the time when people had to push a button several times to find the letter they needed for a word they couldn't spell anyway, but I think I understood some of it.
I am a sheap (sheep), a idot (an idiot) I need to go to skole (school), my moter shoud have swallowed me, I am ovlasy brian ded (obviously brain-dead, I think) and I am a (insert that word I have never in my life been able to say or write).

I acknowledged that they were entitled to voice their uneducated opinion of a person they have never met and know absolutely nothing about, and asked why they hadn't answered the clearly simple questions I had asked.
I went off to make a coffee and when I came back and removed a cat that was sitting on my phone I saw the replies were almost as long as my arm. I skimmed through them, several were in capitals, all were abusive, and most were unreadable. I thought for a while and watched as two more pockets of abuse popped onto the screen. Then I remembered something else I had once read and left one more comment. "You know, it's kind of sad, watching you lot trying to fit your entire vocabulary into one badly written comment." And then I left it. The sad thing is that the idiots wouldn't even understand what I meant.

******

March drifted into April and Stuart had a birthday. His 70th. He had told me that he liked milk chocolate so I bought him three bars to go with a card. He also got a card from a son from his first marriage and Ruth bought him a cake. Well, actually he bought it as he pays for everything, but she picked it up from the shelf during the weekly shop. She also gave him a present. Some juice for his vape thing. Actually it was just half of what she had bought for herself, but she had wrapped it up nicely. I felt sorry for him. I also wondered about the single card from England. I don't expect many cards on my birthday because no one usually knows where I am and I tend to keep birthdays quiet anyway. But this was his 70th, and he had a home with an address, I would have thought he would have had a card or two. But there was nothing.
I realized why a few days later.

Stuart was sitting in the corner of the garden when I went out to join him. I had my phone in my hand because I was planning on reading later, and I have reading books as well as audio books on my phone. As well as music, movies and just about everything I might need. (Oh if only we had had Internet in the 80's, my rucksack would have been so much smaller and lighter and Karen and I would not have had to share tapes as well as clothes).

Knowing the WiFi wouldn't reach the garden Stuart said, "You won't get Facebook out here."

I like Facebook and I usually visit it every day. It's nice to see what people are up to and if I want to tell everyone something I only have to say it once and most people I know will read it eventually. I can share photos, and see the photos of friends and family from the other side of the world. With some friends it's almost like having a long and constant conversation that I can walk away from and get back to later. Most of the people on my friends list are people I know, people I knew before Facebook and who I have actually spent time with. Of course there are cousins and family on the other side of the world who I have never met, and Facebook is a good way to get to know them a little. But mostly I have to have met someone and consider them worthy before I will accept a friend request.

I understand that some people don't do this, that they really have no idea who is reading what they write or who might be masturbating over their photos.

 "I know," I replied and before I could say anything else he told me how I shouldn't mess about with that crap anyway. I wondered if he had been taking bossy lessons from Ruth.

"I had a Facebook once and I had to delete it, it was full of shit." He told me.

"It's only full of shit if your friends are full of shit." I said.

"They are not your friends."

"Mine are."

"You don't know those people," he said.

"Yes I do."

"They are not your friends, you don't know them; they could be anybody."

"I do know them," I said.

"No you don't, friends are people you can see in real life, people you can touch."

"Yes, and people you can add to your friends list on Facebook."

"You don't meet Facebook friends. They are not real." He was getting quite angry for some reason so I stopped responding. I sipped my coffee and wondered how much quiet should be allowed before I could look at my phone and find out what Jack Reacher was up to without being rude. And while I sat there I began to think.

Stuart had no friends.

There was no one but family who he could have had as Facebook friends because there was no one but family who bothered with him. And even then, only one of his two children bothered. I had been in this house for over a month and there had been no phone calls other than from his son; no messages other than the council WhatsApp group that the entire village was expected to be a member of. No birthday cards, no calls or messages of congratulations or good wishes except from his son's children. No one had told him "We'll go for a beer to celebrate when this is over." I believe there is a sister somewhere, but he hadn't heard from her. Before the lockdown I had seen him sitting in the coffee shop (and kept quiet about it because he had told Ruth he was going to the doctors) but he had sat alone. They had both told me how Lockdown made very little difference to them because they hardly went out anyway, and no one came to visit.

He had no friends. Not one.

I doubted if she did either.

The only calls she had were from her father and sister. The only calls she made were to these two people. Neither Stuart nor Ruth ever spoke of anyone else because there was no one else in their lives to speak of. I think I was the only friend the two of them had, and I was learning not to like them. Well, if I'm honest, I liked him. He might not be the sharpest tool in the box, but neither am I. At least he wasn't normally rude. I thought he might be lonely and that was where this little temper tantrum had come from.

This couple had been together for 38 years. She had been little more than a teenager – a very pretty teenager, and he had been a handsome divorcee with two kids. They had originated from Wolverhampton but lived in London for years, both working full time for most of their lives. Yet they had no friends. They talked about things they had done together in the past, or places they had been and holidays they had had, but the only other people who were ever mentioned were family. Not once did I ever hear either of them say "My friend so-and-so….." or "I was with my friend…"

They had bought this house in this tiny Spanish village for next to nothing about 20 years previously and only he had bothered to learn to speak the language. They had both cut themselves off from everyone they had ever met, except me. And, looking back, I realized that any communication we had ever had since leaving Cornwall was when I had made the first move. When she had boasted that they never leave the house she hadn't been joking. He may have wandered around the village and tried to chat to people, I think he had tried to make friends, but she refused to bother. And he had given up. She might be content to live a solitary life bossing him about. But he was lonely. They had never married and now even slept in separate rooms. I had seen no affection between them. They were housemates, nothing more. And he was lonely.

As I sat there, pretending to read but actually thinking, I realized something else. He must really love her with all his heart to have stayed with her for so long.

Either that or he just didn't have the balls to get up and leave.

CHAPTER FOUR

I read that 4000 people had died of Covid-19 in the UK and thousands more were ill, and people were still roaming the streets in groups, going to the beach and taking the kids to the park. All while nothing but tumbleweed rolled around this little village. Via Facebook I asked everyone I knew if they knew of anyone who had had this virus and nobody did. Not one person could say "Yes, I know someone who has it or had it." I didn't know whether to feel lucky or suspicious.
Then one friend's mother died. She was 98 and had been in a care home for ten years not understanding who her own daughters were. Apparently she died of Covid-19 even though she hadn't been ill with anything other than dementia and old age, and cancer.
I am not a conspiracy theorist by any means. But I couldn't help wondering about stuff.

I thought that if a virus was about we were all going to get it anyway, because there was no way not to get it. We had been told to wash our hands more often and stay away from people we didn't live with. Staying home would not only prevent stupid accidents that would clog up the hospitals, but also keep us safe from the virus.
I doubted that.

For instance…

We would go shopping. We would put on our face masks and take our bags and get in the car. Ruth and I would sit in the back where the silver screening on the windows allowed us to see out but prevented others from seeing in. So we were fairly confident of not getting caught. (Only one person was allowed out of the house unless someone had to take a child or a pensioner to the doctor). Once at the next village we would use two shops that were quite close together. Leaving Stuart in the car Ruth would go into one shop and I would go into the other. Then we would swap shops. That way we both got everything we needed while the shops thought we were each on our own, and Ruth got to use Stuart's bank card without him seeing how much she spent. She bought so much chocolate that she ran out of hiding places and I even found it in the cutlery draw. She always insisted that she never ate chocolate so she had to hide it in places she thought Stuart wouldn't go. I caught him rummaging amongst the towels in the bathroom once and watched as he pulled out some chocolate eggs. He offered me one but I hesitated saying "She's probably counted them."

"No," he said shaking his head, "She can't tell us off because she can't admit that they are there." We had two each before he put them back.

But, going into a shop involved sanitizing our hands and putting on the gloves provided. We would do our shopping and then remove the gloves once out of the shop. I guess this was an attempt at keeping the shop safe, but while people had those gloves on their sanitized hands they would also hold onto their own bags that they brought in. They would get out their shopping lists that they wrote at home, put their gloved hands in their pockets, scratch their ears, get out their phone to call someone and make sure they got the right product and generally continue to spread any germs they had all over the place.

Then they got to the cash desk, where someone they didn't know touched every single item either without gloves on, or with gloves on that they had possibly worn for several hours. Some people would then put their gloved hands into their pockets or handbags to get out a bank card to wave at a machine, and some would rest this contactless thing on the machine while they packed their goods away.
I used cash.
And nobody cared.
Money is now, and always has been, possibly the most germ ridden thing on the planet and yet people pass it from hand to hand and then assume that because at least one of them is wearing gloves they are both safe. They probably are, there's likely to be so many other germs on that cash that Covid can't find a space to latch on.
 I was pretty convinced that the only things that could possibly have a chance of staying germ free were the sanitized hands that were still inside the gloves.
I watched what happened with the three of us after we left the shop.
Ruth and I would put the bags of germ covered shopping in the car and Stuart would drive us all home. Then, while he fussed about with keys we would get the bags out of the car and carry them into the house.
The bags would be put down and then unpacked. Ruth would wash her hands before unpacking but I saw no point in that. Why carry a bag full of possible germs then put it down to wash your hands just to pick that same bag up again? As I put my cheese in the fridge I wondered who had touched it, with what, and was that plastic pouch really safe to have around my food anyway? And why was I worrying about germs with all the preservatives now in our food and while I was in a house that stank of cat pee?

I guess it's not possible to have a smell free house when there are four cats living there, even if it is as huge as this one. (Actually it is and I know several people who do just that) But why people with gardens have to have litter trays inside I just don't understand. And there were so many rooms in this house that I couldn't understand why said tray had to be in the living room! The massive living room was the main room in the house and apart from the two bedrooms, it was the whole of the front part of the downstairs. It accommodated the huge front door, a stair case, which had a bathroom underneath it, the pathway once used by the horses to get to the stable, the huge and ancient doors to the patio that was once a courtyard and part of the horse route, the massive fireplace that once housed the ovens and now dwarfed the large wood burner as well as the entrances to the two downstairs bedrooms and the breakfast/dining room. Only the horse route was clear of furniture and even that was lined with chairs and tables and cupboards and some sort of small church organ. On the other side of the route stood more tables and chairs and cupboards as well as two huge sofas and a giant TV that somehow still managed to look lost in the corner. And the entire place stank of cat pee and poo. You could smell it as soon as you stepped though the normal sized door that had been cut into one of the giant front doors. The litter tray sat by the patio doors but the cats didn't bother with it much. Most of them just seemed to go where they liked. I had come out of my room one morning to find Gail squatting by the front door and told Ruth, but she said I must be wrong because Gail wouldn't do that. Apparently only Maggie didn't bother with the tray and she only pooped upstairs. I found that as long as I kept my bedroom window open it didn't smell in there at least. I think even Thomas got fed up with the smell because he was always trying to get inside my room. I would have let him in but I wasn't allowed to. Most mornings I found him sitting on one of the small tables outside my door and if I didn't great him as soon as I came out he would swipe a paw at me as I walked past.

Thomas really was the best of the four. He was the most sociable and the only one who liked to play. Roll up a ball of tinfoil and Thomas was happy for hours. Leave a cardboard box on the floor and he would get inside it and hide till dinner time. Put a book down absolutely anywhere and he would find it and sit on it. He once sat on my puzzle book as I was trying to solve one of the puzzles, pushing my hand out of his way with his paw. If I sat in the patio or the garden he would come and sit by my feet. When I came in from my morning walks he would run across the room to greet me, and almost every morning I would find him waiting for me as I came out of my room.

Maggie would sit on my lap if I was on the sofa, but I think that was mainly because I was in her spot and she didn't give a toss. She was going to sit in her spot whether it was vacant or not. Linda would usually be around somewhere asking for attention, and food. I would usually give her some ham even though Ruth told me not to as the cats were not allowed to have processed food. I have no idea what Ruth thought I was eating or what she thought came out of those tins and pouches she fed to the cats, or what the treats were made of, or the cheese that she would give Linda every day, I just continued to slide tidbits onto the floor when she wasn't looking.

Gail never came anywhere near me. She would only crouch and stare at me as if I were the devil before running off in a panic.

As the weather warmed up I spent less and less time in the living room, I just couldn't cope with the smell and I was sure there was something living in one of the sofas because I always seemed to get bitten when I sat there. Instead I started to spend my evening in the patio either reading or watching YouTube.

And then one of the cats escaped from next door.

Just as Gail had done before him, this ginger tom had found his way first to the roof tops of one of those half finished rooms, and then over the roof of the empty building behind. From there he walked along the top of a wall and then onto one of the upper terraces of this house. For the first day he simply sat on the terrace and stared down at us in the garden. Then he started crying. Stuart left some food up there, but they were not going to encourage the cat to stay.
The second time he showed up Ruth and I were looking up at him when I said "Maybe he's trying to tell us something. Maybe he wants help."
"How do you know it's a he?" she asked.
"I've seen him from behind," I said. "There's no mistake."
We watched as he mewed at us then Ruth said. "I think he's trying to tell us something."
I had nicknamed him Biscuit because he's ginger and because I had seen him from behind, but I got told not to be so stupid. She was not having a cat with a stupid name like that. "It's OK," I had said, "He's not your cat."
As we looked up at him that day he decided to turn his back on us. "Oh my God, just look at the nuts on that!" announced Ruth. But she still refused to refer to him as Biscuit. In fact, from that day on he was known as Ginger Nuts, or just Nuts. I suggested that we check on the other cat next door and for once Ruth agreed with me and off we went.

It was then proved that this other cat was defiantly female because Biscuit/Ginger Nuts had left her with a couple of crumbs. The problem was that as soon as I spotted them the mother shot off and hid. Ruth and I left the house to fetch some decent cat food and hoped that she would use that time to go back and fetch her babies. And that is exactly what she did. So we left the food and hoped that everything would be OK. Ginger Nuts had done his share of raising his young, he had told us they existed and from that moment they were no longer his problem. (No, I'm sorry; I still can't call him that. From here on I will call him Ginger, although his name was defiantly to be Nuts, even long after they had been removed.)

For the following few days Ginger continued to come to the terrace and mew at us and Stuart found a way of feeding him up there without Ruth finding out. Then the cat disappeared for a couple of days and I thought he had found somewhere else to live.
But then he came back.
From his perch on the terrace we could see that he had been hurt. He had a cut on his leg and a blood around his mouth. It looked to the three of us as if he had fallen from a great height and landed on his face rather than his feet.
But that wasn't going to be Ruth's problem. He was a cat and was capable of looking after himself, and she had her own cats to worry about. She didn't need any more vets bills. Besides, Gail was in season again so a tom was not welcome.

Stuart was alone in the garden when Ginger finally made his way to the ground by jumping six feet onto the barbed wire atop a wall, and then over a huge cactus, to land on some giant stones that had been laid over a drain to prevent it from getting blocked. The fact that I found marks in the dirt where Stuarts ladder had been had absolutely nothing to do with it, neither did the fact that the ladder was dropping dirt as he took it *from* the stable again to remove the barbed wire 'just in case'. And, of course, it was not his decision to suddenly find his lost credit card so Gail could be taken to the vet as she was almost constantly in season. Neither was it Stuart's fault that a brand new box of cat flea and tick treatment just happened to be found lurking at the back of his medicine shelf when he got back from the vet. Ruth was suspicious about the flea and tick treatment, but I really don't think she ever knew about the ladder marks. She was adamant that Ginger was not coming into the house and she even made up a bed for him in the garden, and under the terrace so he wouldn't get wet if it rained. Stuart also made the cat a bed in the back room and he 'forgot' to lock the cat flap in the garden door each night. Stuart also found some antibiotics at the back of that same shelf, and I wandered into the kitchen one day to find Ruth holding Ginger down while Stuart forced a pill into the cat's mouth.
"It's for his face and leg" Ruth offered.
 "Oh, did the vet prescribe pills without seeing him?" I tried not to sound disbelieving.
"No," said Stuart, "They are antibiotics that we had for Thomas last year, he didn't need them all."
I kept quiet, I said nothing. There would be no point at all in explaining to these people how antibiotics work. That you must finish the course even if you are a cat, and that they cannot be kept and given to someone else – even if it is another cat – a year later. But Stuart was convinced that one or maybe two of these year old pills would heal the poor cats face.

I was pleased to see him throw them up in the garden a few minute later.

It was three days before Ginger was allowed the run of the house and Stuart was making another appointment at the vet. Ruth and I went back to look for the kittens but couldn't find them. Then Ruth announced that it didn't take two of us to look for them nor to feed them so I was dismissed. I did not go next door again until it was necessary. It was made clear to me that I was not to have anything to do with Ginger and I should keep my mouth shut about his now healing injuries and I was not to give him any ham from my lunch.

****

Life continued to drag.
My cousin in Norfolk went shopping in Norwich and complained about the amount of traffic. She said that most of the shops were actually open and the place was almost as busy as normal. One friend in Exmouth complained that the beach was packed and another moaned that he had forgotten get something from the DIY shop before it closed for Easter. I saw a Facebook post saying that social distancing was now over and everyone was getting back to normal and another that said she had been stopped by the police and asked where she was going. She claimed to have told the policeman that she was 'goin out' and that he had asked her to go home. She claimed to have told him to 'F*uck off' as she drove away. It seems the police in England could only suggest that someone go home if they had no reason to be out and, of course, lots of idiots were claiming to have told them where to get off (or Tol then wre to get of – to quote one). But in Spain the police would instruct you to go home while allowing you a view of the gun at their belt. Although I did hear that there had been some riots in Madrid we saw nothing of that in our tiny village.

I felt quite lucky to be in Spain. I may have had to put up with Ruth telling me not to forget my mask every time I went within six feet of the front door, but at least I didn't have to put up with the kind of fool that was on the loose back home.

I wondered about this virus and how it could be a good thing. If it killed off lots of people in England I might be in with a chance of a better job when I got home. I liked all three of the jobs I had, but one of them was changing and I knew it was about to get very difficult. I was in two minds as to whether I really wanted to go back to it. I had promised someone that I would not let someone else down, but I knew it was going to be hard. I wondered if there was any chance the virus would kill off certain people and make my life a lot easier. I daydreamed of going back to empty villages and quiet cities; of driving on almost empty roads and of being able to walk on empty beaches. We've all seen TV programs about what could happen if enough of the population was wiped out and I almost started to look forward to it. To go back to a time where there was enough work for everyone; enough food and plenty of empty buildings so no one had to sleep outside in the cold and rain. I've always been grateful I wasn't around for the Black Death, but I have to admit that it had its advantages. Mother Nature keeps sending us all these killer bugs to try and cull the population but, like the lice on a school kids head, we keep on living. One hundred years ago a virus tried to wipe out all the young and strong, and it killed more people than the First World War. But Covid-19 seemed to be getting at the very old and vulnerable more than the young and healthy. This seemed, to me at least, like a more sensible cull. I just hoped that I survived it. Along with my son, of course, and my siblings, and cousins, and my aunts and uncles, and everyone else I cared about.
I looked at Ruth and wondered how selective this virus could be.

After the vet bills went onto the credit card Ruth upped her moaning. I'm not quite sure why as she had explained to me how Stuart paid for everything because she was too young to retire and not able to work in Spain. I had agreed that it wasn't easy for a foreigner who wasn't qualified for a fancy job and got a lecture on how she was qualified, actually, in lots of things, actually. She was qualified to work in a bank and had, in fact, been a supervisor; she was a qualified hairdresser and had, in fact, been qualified to train people to do this job, had been in charge of the bloody collage department, actually; she was a qualified retail manager and had, in fact, spent most of her working life as area manager for a well known furniture chain in England. I did not ask her why, then, she had been working in a charity shop when I first met her, and for all the time I had known her. And I have never admitted that I know the real reason why she 'left'. But she carried on, spending a fair amount of time moaning about having to save money while consistently wasting it.

There is a well in this garden. Stuart drew the water up for me several times because it comes from an underground river and tastes better than what comes out of the tap. And it doesn't smell like a swimming pool. Had this been my house the first thing I would have done would have been to rig up some sort of pulley to make it easier to get the water up in a bucket. I would then have used it as much as possible. But here we were not allowed to use it because Ruth says tap water is better. So the well stays covered and a tap to the mains has been fitted to the wall right next to it to use while watering the garden.

There is a solar panel to heat the water during the day, so I had assumed I would be expected to have my shower in the evening. I had assumed wrong. I was expected to have my shower in the morning after the eclectic heater had been on. And even though there were lashings of hot water in the evening, a kettle was usually boiled to do the washing up. And while washing up in one sink in the double unit, the tap is left running in the other sink for rinsing. I didn't ask about her methods of saving money, I didn't want to hear the answers.

The whole water heating system was odd anyway. The boiler and solar panel heated the water in a tank that was so far away from any shower that the water was lukewarm by the time it got there and this was after running the shower for roughly five minutes to get the cold out of the pipes. During these five minutes all that water went down the drain and yes, there was a water meter. Had I lived there alone I would have saved that water in buckets to flush the toilet or water the garden.

Or I would have had the tank moved to avoid the problem in the first place.

Or had some sort of instant heat system fitted.

I discovered later that Stuart and Ruth had actually had both bathrooms and the water system fitted to the house. It seems they may have designed it this way!

Right by the well there is an old horse trough that is now used for washing shoes and anything too dirty for the kitchen sink. I once went to use it to wash my shoes and was told to use the water from the tap next to it. There was a hose attached to the tap so I was pleased to be able to use the hot water that had been heated in the sun while sitting in the hose pipe and later I suggested using this water to wash up, as said hose pipe was just outside the window over the sink. This resulted in my receiving a lecture on germs. And then, one day, I saw Stuart running this hot water down the drain because he needed cold to water the plants. I just couldn't understand their way of thinking.

"You know what I'd do if I lived here alone?" I asked Stuart once while we were sitting in the patio and Ruth was banging things about in the kitchen.

"What?"

"I'd fill that horse trough with water from the well in the morning and let the sun heat it during the day, and then I'd have my bath in there in the evening."

"That's what I do when she's not around." he told me, "She won't let me do it when she's here, she says it's not right for some reason. But that's why I paint the bottom of it. So it's smooth to sit on." The more I talked to Stuart the more I liked him.

Stuart would often tell me stories from his past and I usually ended up laughing. If his stories were made up then he is a very clever man and should be a writer, but I actually think they are mostly true. Especially the ones about his grandfather who fought in the Boar war and WW1. Stuart told me how his grandfather would make tea while away at war by pushing his tin helmet into the muddy ground until water started to dribble over the rim. By doing this he could collect enough water, with as little dirt as possible, to make a mug of tea. If they had any tea. Most of the time they would just boil the muddy water and pretend it was tea because it was about the right colour anyway. This old man had also said that one time he had been following a cart somewhere during the Boar war and he had looked down to see that they were walking on bodies. There were so many of them and they had been there so long that they had become molded into the ridges of the road. The cart wheels had literally left ridges in the bodies. The old man said he could see uniform buttons and pockets. Stuart had one grandfather who had been something of a hero, surviving both the Boar War and WW1, while the other grandfather seemed to have been a bit of a joker. This old man had a wooden leg and according to Stuart it was just like a table leg like you see in the cartoons. (Or at least we used to see in cartoons; with today's feeble society I doubt a wooden leg would be allowed in a cartoon now). Stuart had no idea how the leg was attached only that his grandfather was treated with respect because everyone thought he had lost his leg in the war. But in fact he had lost it at the age of 16 when a cut had become infected and it had been amputated to save his life. This grandfather had never been to war.

CHAPTER FIVE

I had thought the daily announcements were loud but I knew nothing about noise until Easter Sunday. I really was not prepared to be woken that early on a Sunday morning by cannon fire that sounded as if it were right outside my window. In fact it was possibly on the other side of the village, but as each skinny street is lined with terraced houses of at least three stories high the noise bounces between walls like a high powered rubber ball on speed. By the time it reached my window it had so many echoes that I thought I was at Waterloo. I lay there wondering how many of the 17 bedrooms were left next door and how many had been blown to Benidorm when I heard another noise. As the echoes died away I opened my bedroom door to allow a spiky ginger thing resembling a cross between the Tasmanian Devil and a porcupine into the room. Thomas threw himself under my bed and tried to get under the rug as well. I sat on the floor and talked to him until his eyes shrank to normal size and his spikes became fir once more. Eventually he came and sat on the bed with me.

Then the church bells started.

And they seemed to go on all day. I wasn't sure if church services were allowed but, being atheist, I didn't really care.

I managed to sneak Thomas out of my room without getting caught and he ran upstairs to hide elsewhere. I had my shower and went into the kitchen to find the other cats not in the least bit bothered by the bells that were still ringing. Ginger and Gail were sitting on the counter top and Linda and Maggie were at the food trays. There was food in the trays. There was always food in the trays. But this was last night's food and they had no intention of touching it. I wasn't going to touch it either, I was going to hold my nose as I went to the fridge and I was going to try not to step in it as I opened the door. For Heaven's sake, I thought, litter trays in the living room and food trays on the floor by the fridge door! Add that to the piss that was constantly soaking its way through the concrete floor of the horse route and the stink of a new tom cat in the house and I almost didn't bother with breakfast.
Then Ginger jumped down from the counter top and sprayed the plates that were on the shelf below.

This kitchen is long and not too wide. All along one side there are storage units. Three big ones, with the middle one having draws under the counter. The other two have shelves. No doors, just shelves where all the plates and bowls, saucepans and general kitchen things are kept. I had once counted six different dinner sets on those shelves, some with enough for twelve settings. There were more sets in the cupboards in the Breakfast/dining room, the living room and the back room. I have no idea why two people need so many plates, but there they sat, covered in dust and now cat pee. I took a dusty plate from a pile I thought might be safe, sniffed it for evidence of cat, washed it anyway and made my breakfast.

When Ruth finally came down I was washing the pile of plates and I explained why. I suggested that we wash all the other piles as well, just in case, but Ruth didn't think that was necessary. She said she couldn't smell anything and anyway, Ginger was going to the vet soon so he would stop spraying after that. I was grateful that I cooked my own food because it meant that I could choose my own plate, and wash it before I used it! Ruth told me that she had bought some disinfectant and if I saw the cat spraying again I was to spray over it with the disinfectant. I thought that perhaps a bucket of hot soapy water might be a better idea, but hey, it's not my house, so I kept quiet.

Ruth and I sat in the breakfast/dining room drinking our coffee while looking at our phones. I was reading something and she asked what it was.
"English news," I said, "People are complaining because they can't go to church" I wondered how many of them were actually religious and how many just wanted to make a fuss.
She Huffed. "What rubbish site are you reading that on? You always read crap."
"Oh, I thought The Guardian would be quite reasonable."
"That's not The Guardian."
"It says so at the top."
She looked over at my phone and huffed again. I glanced at hers and saw that she was reading the Spanish news in English.
She then decided to ask about my ferry home.
"When is your ferry will you make it?"
"On the 24th, and no, I won't."
"Why not?"
I looked at her; she was seriously asking this stupid question and wanting an answer.
I said, "Because I cannot leave this house, there is no way for me to get across the country, the Portuguese border is closed and my van doesn't have an engine."

"I thought your friend had fixed it."
"He got the engine out but now he can't finish it yet."
"Well, tell him to get it done, you need it."
"Ruth, he can't. Portugal is in lockdown the same as here, their rules are very strict, he is not allowed to work."
"The garages in England are open."
"Raymond isn't in England, he is in Portugal, and the rules are different. He doesn't work on emergency vehicles so he has been told to close."
"But your van is an ambulance."
"Yes, but it's an English ambulance, in use as a camper van, it is not essential. Certainly not in Portugal."
I tried to change the subject by telling her that I had cancelled the ferry so she demanded to know what I had done that for.
"Because I'm not going to make it, so I had no choice but to let them know."
"Well, that was stupid; you've lost your money now. You should have waited till they cancelled it like the airline, then you would have got your money back."
"No, they are not going to cancel it because they are still running."
"No they are fucking not!" She almost bit my head off. "All the ferries are cancelled, nothing is running. You've lost your money."
"I don't know about the other ferries but P&O are still running between Dover and Calais and I have been told I'll get a voucher to use later."
"You should never have called them, you won't get a voucher, you need something in writing."
Trying to stay calm I said, "I didn't call, I emailed, I got a response and I have a voucher number. It's all sorted."
"Pth!" was her only response.

A couple of days later I finally heard from the British embassy. I emailed them back and explained my situation and told them that I wasn't sure if I would be able to stay in that house until legally allowed to leave. If Ruth was hinting at my leaving I was afraid she could explode at any point and I was worried she would tell me to leave.

Ye gods I wanted to leave. Not only did I contact the embassy but I also contacted the border force and begged them to let me know as soon as they could when the border would reopen. Every day I checked the internet for news of what was happening and every day I checked the airline website, and the trains and busses, just in case there was anything moving. But there was nothing. I even learned that there were smuggler routs in and out of Portugal and I found three of them on my map. But further research told me that they would be impossible to use even if I could get there.

I was stuck.

******

I decided to clean my room again and wash my sheets. I put them in the machine early in the morning and hung them on the line when the machine finished about lunch time. Ruth later took them off the line and they disappeared upstairs. So much for my being allowed to keep them in my room for the following week. I wondered if this was a sign that she planned on throwing me out by the following week. I put the other sheets on the bed and went to the cleaning cupboard for polish and dusters. I had to ask what to use because the furniture is antique and I didn't want to spoil anything. So I stood quietly seething as the method of using a spray polish was explained to me. I began to imagine what she would tell people about me after I left. 'She's so stupid I even had to explain how to use a spray polish'. But I realized there was only her sister and her father to tell, she has no friends. And surely they must know her well enough to know what she is like. Unless arrogance was hereditary.

Then she explained the vacuum cleaner. I had wanted it to vacuum the rug but Ruth explained the vacuum would not do this in the normal way. "It's too suhky" she said.

"Sorry, it's what?"

"Too suhky"

I still didn't get it, but you must remember that she has a strong Wolverhampton accent and although I live in Cornwall, I am from Norfolk.

Ruth explained the term 'too suhky'. (Sucky)

What she actually meant was that the suction on the vacuum was very strong and it will try and suck up the carpet. Therefore I must use the hose pipe. She explained how and where to attach the pipe and told me to be sure to vacuum under the bed to stop the ants getting in. Now I really was confused.

"Ants?"

"Yes, if you don't vacuum under the bed properly the ants will get under the door."

I gave up on that one immediately and asked why, if the vacuum has a strong suction, she didn't alter it by moving the dial.
"What dial?"
"That dial there, it alters the level of the foot so the suction is either…." But I got no further.
"Don't be so bloody stupid, you can't change the suction, use the pipe like I said, and remember to do under the bed". And in typical Ruth fashion, she walked away.
I took the vacuum to the bedroom, altered the dial and vacuumed the rug without using the pipe. I then pushed the other button so the handle lay almost flat to the floor and I pushed the whole thing under the bed. I still have no idea how cleaning under the bed will stop ants from getting in under the door, but I had learned to just keep quiet and do as I was told.
Maybe Ruth keeps chocolate under her bed.

I was putting the vacuum back in the cupboard when I heard shouting coming from the garden.
"I like it, leave it there"
"Well I fucking hate it so get it down."
"You get it down."
"No, you get it down."
A cactus, they were arguing over a cactus. I stood in the doorway watching this childishness for a minute and then I slid quietly back into the house hoping I had not been spotted. As I did so I heard Ruth getting the upper hand.
"The cats will get hurt," she shouted.
"The cats won't go anywhere near it."
"Nuts did, I saw him, he was trying to find a way out and he was trying to fucking climb up it to get to the top of the wall."
Well that was something new, I had never heard of a cat climbing a cactus before.

I heard footsteps so I turned to look as if I had just that very second walked into the back room from the kitchen. I watched as Stuart came in from the garden and turned right into the stable at the other side of this back room. As I stepped into the garden he came out behind me carrying something that resembled a samurai sword. The cactus was hacked to pieces and removed, watched by the gloating Ruth. She knew she had won because she knew Stuart would not risk a cat being hurt and, although he still denied it, she knew he wanted to keep Ginger.
While he chopped away the two of them continued to argue with him saying he wanted to keep part of it, and her, standing with hands on hips, saying it all had to go. The result was that it was all removed and chopped up with most of it being put into huge buckets that Ruth and I then took to the communal bin at the end of the street once she had dresses and put on her make up. The rest was left in a pile because it was apparently going to go where the sun doesn't shine.
Stuart and I were then informed that Ruth doesn't need to be told anything because she already knows, and there is nothing she can learn from a know-it-all like him; and anyway, he is ignorant and what the fuck was I laughing at?
"Nothing," I said, "I was just thinking; Ginger can't get out now so you'll have to keep him."
Ruth snorted and left the garden.
Stuart sat and smiled to himself.

My legs had started aching. It was an ache I recognized as one that appears if I have forgotten to take a daily pill. But I hadn't forgotten so I looked at the bottle and immediately saw the problem. While I was meant to take 300mg a day these ones from the local pharmacy were only 50mg. I would need six of these things a day so I decided to go back to the pharmacy to find some stronger ones. As I headed for the front door I heard the usual cry of "Don't forget your mask" and responded with my usual cry of "I'm wearing it." I stepped through the door from the dark chill of the house into the bright sunshine and blazing heat of the Spanish Springtime. I shut the door behind me and stood still for a moment, loving the feel of the sun on my skin and wondering how long it was safe to stand there before being reduced to cinders. I was getting up earlier and earlier to do my daily exercise walk so as to be back inside before it got too hot, but a slow stroll was fine and I enjoyed my wander to the centre of the village; in the next street.

All four shops were shut.

The butcher, the baker, the minimarket and the pharmacy were all closed and with their shutters down. The place was silent and empty. I stood in the middle of the road in the very hub of the village and saw no movement and heard no sound. It was even too hot for the birds. It was surreal, nothing moved. I wondered if my dream had come true and the rest of the population was dead. I had only felt that feeling once before, in the south of Italy the year before. I had stumbled upon what I assumed must have been a holiday village, empty because it was still early in the year. There I had seen bikes rusting in gardens, awnings torn from over patio doors and flapping in the wind, and grass growing along the pavements and roads. I had left that village because it was just too freaky, and I felt a bit like that now, as I stood in the middle of the road in this tiny village in Spain. Except this village was still cared for.

I sauntered back to the house, seeing no one at all, hearing nothing, not even the distant rumble of a vehicle on the duel carriageway. I stepped inside and took off my mask. I hung it on a chair back and sprayed it with alcohol as directed by the pharmacist when I had bought the 'non disposable' new edition to normal outdoor wear. Then I wandered into the breakfast/dining room.
"Did you get it ok?" asked Ruth.
"No, they were shut, I'll go back……"
"They are not fucking shut!"
"Yes they are, they all……"
"No they are not, it's Monday; nothing shuts on Mondays."
"It must be a saint day or something because everything is shut."
She got up to look at her wall calendar and then announced that it wasn't a saint day or she would have it written down. I was wrong and she would show me I was wrong. She leaned over to the shelf where she kept her makeup and grabbed the bag. She did her face and went off to get dressed; in that order so I assumed it wasn't her day for a shower.
She came back a few minutes later and sprayed herself with perfume. As two of the cats gagged and fled to the safety of the garden she told me she had a new bank card to activate so she was going out to do that and she would find out that the shops were not all shut after all.
She stomped off towards the door muttering about how stupid I am. She unlocked the door, opened it and stepped outside. I heard the door close again and I waited.
I heard the door open again and she stomped back through the living room to where I stood holding her facemask by the ear straps. Silently I handed it to her and she snatched it then stomped back towards the door once more.
I took my coffee to the back garden to sit in the shade of the terrace above with Linda at my feet. When Thomas jumped on my lap I could still smell the chemical essence of the cheap perfume Ruth had sprayed.

Ten minutes later she was back and now she really was angry. Linda didn't hang around for that, she took off and chased Maggie back into the house while Thomas ran for the stable. "It must be a saint day" she said and then demanded of Stuart why there had been no announcement. While she talked, telling us how there was always an announcement and she didn't know why there hadn't been one this morning, or why there had been nothing in the news online and she didn't understand why everything had to close on a Monday, Stuart and I simply sat and sipped our coffees and said nothing. And I wondered why the hell it mattered to her because she never normally even leaves the house anyway.

****

A decision was made about the new cat. The one I called Ginger and Ruth called Nuts; the one they were not going to keep. Even though Gail had now been spade and had recovered and was finally quiet, Stuart thought it would be a good idea for Ginger to be 'sorted' as well. Ruth had previously told me that he would be going to the vet but now it was Stuart who thought it was his idea. So finally there was something they both agreed on.
Almost.
 Stuart was sure that the real owner should be told what was going on and I heard him tell Ruth to send the woman a text and explain that the cat had been living with them for a while and that he would pay the vets bills if he could keep it. I then heard Ruth tell Stuart that she didn't need him to tell her what to say, that she wasn't daft, she knew how to talk and how to send a text message and she didn't need his bloody help with anything. Later she showed me the message she had sent and I saw that it was quite clear. The owner was irresponsible for leaving the cats alone in the yard and she was to pay for the operation to prevent other cats from having kittens.

Ruth even showed me the response that came half an hour later.

The woman was sorry for the trouble and would certainly pay for the operation and she would have both cats removed from the house as soon as possible.

As I was reading it Stuart asked Ruth if there had been a response.

I gave her the phone back and left them to it.

From my room I could hear nothing, not even a raised voice. But later Ruth went to bed for the afternoon, which was something she had not done before, and when she got up she was as nice as could be to both Stuart and myself. Ginger was not to become their cat. He was to be removed along with his sister and their kittens, provided they could get him back into the house next door, and it was Ruth's fault. I think that for once in her life, she knew she was wrong. She knew she had messed up. Stuart was so angry with her that he wouldn't even speak.

I took full advantage of her absence during that afternoon and I cooked a couple of meals to go in the fridge and be heated up later.

I like plane boring food and I love mashed potato but the one time I had cooked it there I had got into trouble. Ruth had walked passed just as the lid lifted from the pot and a dribble of water bubbled out over the rim. I immediately lifted the lid and turned down the heat and the dribble evaporated against the side of the hot pan. But it was too late. She had seen it and I got a lecture on why I shouldn't be allowed to boil potatoes. I was informed that I should not have had the lid on in the first place because lids cause the water to boil over, and I had let the water boil all over the fucking place. If I were to let that happen again I will have fucked up her whole oven and that thing cost a fortune to replace. And anyway, I shouldn't eat potatoes because that was the reason I was so fucking fat, because I eat too many potatoes. She had told me to eat those 'Batatta Brava' things instead. (Which are potatoes, cut into cubes and covered in oil.)

So that afternoon, while she sulked in her room and Stuart watched an old movie in his, I cooked up lots of mashed potatoes and made two cheese and potato pies for myself. And I put the t-towel outside on the line to dry out properly.

This had been one thing that really annoyed and worried me since I had been at this house. That t-towel had been there all along. The same one; used every day for over a month. Allowed to get soaking wet while being wiped over wet dishes and then simply hung back over the draw handle to wait for the next time. It wasn't even what I considered a real t-towel; it was cotton of the type a man's dress shirt would be made from. I felt it was fine for polishing glasses but absolutely useless for drying pots and pans. Granted, in that heat it was dry in no time at all so possibly didn't attract the kind of revolting things a damp towel in England might, but I still felt it should be washed now and again. Especially as we were to use it as an oven glove as well! Ruth had told me that oven gloves were disgusting things that were filled with germs so she refused to have one and it was better to use the t-towel instead. I took the thing from the draw handle and peeled the hand towel from its home over the door under the sink and hung them both out in the sunshine. Really I wanted to set fire to them both but I hoped natures heat would help in some way. I had washed the hand towel once, to be asked why I had interfered. So I hadn't bothered again, I had just stopped using it, preferring to take my own hand towel into the bathroom if I needed to wash my hands.

To hear Ruth talk about my size, as she did on several occasions, anyone would think I was obese. While I agree I was a bit over weight at a size 12-14 and standing just 5 feet tall, I have never thought of myself as 'so fucking fat'. But I had not been insulted, I had just wondered if this creature had ever seen a mirror because she was roughly the same height and size as me except for the fact that my boobs were normal size and in the normal place while hers were enormous and hanging somewhere around her waist causing her to stoop. I had once made the mistake of suggesting that she have a fitting before buying a bra and had been told that she knew her own tits well enough and didn't need any jumped up sales assistant to tell her what to wear. Her back didn't ache because of her bra; it ached because of her age. I didn't bother to point out that she was a year younger than me and my back didn't ache.

****

The Spanish Lockdown was extended again and people in England talked about 'when this is all over' as if that would be sometime next week. My boss was sure the company would be up and running by the middle of May and I knew it wouldn't be because I was actually reading the news most mornings. The Italians were still singing from Balconies and now, apparently, falling in love with neighbors they had previously never known existed and still couldn't reach. All over Europe people were standing in the street clapping to say thank you to their respective hospital workers, and in America they were protesting and claiming they had a right not to wear masks and the government couldn't control them. I saw a photo of a woman holding a placard that said, "Give me freedom or give me Covid" and wondered if she should really be allowed out on her own. Another woman was interviewed on the street somewhere in America and told the reporter that the Coronavirus was Europe's problem and had nothing to do with America, and Facebook was filled with stories of the American president telling people to inject themselves with disinfectant.

I actually searched for that interview and found a clip of it. I saw no evidence of him saying that at all, I only saw him appearing to think out loud and ask something like "I don't know, can that be done?" If the general population can interpret that to mean 'drink bleach and inject yourself with disinfectant' then they possibly need to go ahead and take themselves out of the gene pool. Preferably before they have the chance to breed!

While all this was going on I had a lesson in how to hang my washing out.

I had just hung it out and was about to sit down with my coffee when Ruth said, "Why do you hang your stuff like that?"

"Like what?"

I was then told that I shouldn't hang my dresses by the hem, but by the shoulder so they dry better and I should hang my leggings by the waist band so as not to get peg marks at the bottom of the legs. I wondered about the peg marks at the shoulders of a dress and thought that as my leggings were inside out there would be no visible peg marks anyway, but I said nothing. I was informed that I had obviously never been taught how to do things properly and I should take it all off and do it right. I simply shrugged and said, "It really doesn't matter, it will all be dry in an hour's time anyway."
"No it won't, not there."
I couldn't think what she meant so I stayed quiet and she took that to mean that I was asking so continued with "The sun moves quickly here, it'll be in the shade in a few minutes and it won't dry then. You should have put it at the other end of the line."
"It'll be fine." I said, as if I really didn't care, which I didn't, and I sat down. It was close to thirty degrees, I really didn't think the shade would make much difference.
As I sat there I looked at the washing hanging in front of me. She had told me to peg it at the other end of the line. It was a short line and my washing took up most of it, but there was a larger gap at one end than there was at the other. So the next time I did any washing I started pegging from the other end, only to be told that the sun moves the other way and everything would be in the shade soon and therefore wouldn't dry. And it was still upside down.Both times my laundry had been dried and back in the cupboard within a couple of hours, shade or no shade, and I never did work out which way she thought the sun moved and why it should be quicker there than anywhere else in the world, or how she thought it could change directions.

CHAPTER SIX

One morning I got up with a determination to enjoy the day regardless of any telling off I might get. I had my walk, ate my breakfast and was happily sitting in the walled patio with Thomas at my feet when Ruth came out in her dressing gown. "Morning," she said as Thomas ran for the garden. I thought that was strange because he was her cat, maybe she had just made him jump. But then she sat down next to me.
Do cats have noses like dogs?
I know dogs have a much better sense of smell than humans, but I'm not sure about cats. It would have made a lot of sense to find out they are the same. Because I could smell Ruth as she sat down. It wasn't so much her, as her hair. I think she is fairly cleanish body wise, but I was never sure about her hair. That morning I found out and it really wasn't very nice.

Ruth's hair is very long and very curly. Very 1980's, but natural. I've known, and been jealous of, several people with hair like hers, but I have never been jealous of Ruth. Once, while still in Cornwall, she had told me that there was nothing she could do with it. Absolutely nothing at all. I had mentioned how I knew other people with hair like hers and how they managed it. One has hers straightened and one uses some kind of oil to keep it calm, but I had been informed that Ruth was a hairdresser and she knew that those things don't work. The only thing she could do with it was to leave it lose or tie it back in a lose pony tail. Either way, Ruth usually looks like Catweazle's younger sister. The fact that she was going grey and only ever coloured the front, completely ignoring the back, made it worse. As did the fact that she refused to brush or comb it unless she had just washed it and it was still wet. At this point she would drag a comb through it, ripping out knots and tangles that had been there for days and moaning about how thin it was getting. Since I had been at the house I had learned that she only washed it once every couple of weeks and when she sat down next to me that morning I was grateful she had given up smoking.

She smelled like the hand towel that hung in the kitchen, the one that never got washed. Having cigarette smells attached to that would have been too much to cope with.

Needing to point my nose away from her I looked up and the sky and said the first thing that came into my head. "Look at that sky, so blue it's perfect. It might be a lovely day even though the report is for cloud."

"It's going to rain," she said, "Thunder storms."

"Really?" I asked, "The report just said cloud."

"No it doesn't, it says thunder storms." And she got out her phone.

Knowing what she was doing I got mine out as well. I had been sure it only said cloud just five minutes ago. But Ruth was determined to prove me wrong. We compared weather reports and mine said cloud while hers said thunder storms.

"How strange," she said, while I noticed that we were looking at two totally different companies giving reports for two different areas. But then Ruth must have worked it out because she asked me what area my report was for. I scrolled up and showed her where it gave the name of the village we were in.

"Where's yours for?" I asked. And she gave me the name of the next closest village which was about five miles away.

"Well, maybe they'll get the storm and we'll just get the cloud." I said, hoping to avoid an argument.

I should have known better. I was then told not to be so stupid and that of course whatever they have over there will happen here, you can't have thunder storms in one place and just have cloud in the next village; the weather doesn't work like that. But that, dear reader, is exactly what happened. While we just had a few dark clouds I watched the blackness descend on the neighboring village and later saw the flashes of lightening, although I heard no thunder.

 I sat out in the garden in the shade of one of the terraces the entire afternoon only coming in to make the occasional coffee and then going back to read more about how Alexander the Great was dressing weird and his men were worried about him.

Later that evening Ruth told me that we did have a thunder storm here after all.

"Really?" I asked, wondering how I had missed it while sitting in the garden.

"Yes," she said happily, as if she were proving me wrong once more, "In fact it was quite bad."

I couldn't think of anything to say so I just went to the fridge to see what to have for dinner.

I had been in the garden but even if I had been in the house I would have known if we'd had a thunder storm over head. The house was big, but not so big that I wouldn't have known about a storm at the front just because I was sitting at the back. How could this happen: What was this woman thinking of?
I'd come across this sort of thing a couple of times during my 50something years and it had always confused me. Everyone tells the odd lie now and again, but to lie to someone who knows you are lying; to look at them and know that they know you are lying, and to keep on lying is just incomprehensible. There is absolutely no point, so why do it? As I put my cheese and potato pie in the microwave I knew that Ruth's problems were worse than I had thought.

When I had first met her I had thought she was a bit bossy, but basically nice. She always seemed to want to help people and she seemed to be a huge animal lover.
The first time I had stayed at the house in Spain I had realized that she was actually very bossy and could be quite offensive at times. Like with the incident over the frying pan.

I had had my van then, parked outside in the street with everything I owned inside it. So when I had been given an enormous frying pan to fry just one egg I had gone out and fetched in my tiny one. It's a real frying pan, just very small, and just big enough for one decent egg or two small ones. But Ruth wouldn't allow me to use it in her kitchen.
"It's a real one," I had said, "I means I don't need so much oil or such a big flame and my egg won't be as flat as paper."
"It's a fucking toy and it's not going on my cooker. Use a proper pan." She had retorted. She would not accept that a frying pan with a radius of less than ten inches could possibly be real.

But back then I had decided to simply deal with her attitude and I had left before there was any chance of a real problem. Now I knew she must have some sort of mental disorder. It wasn't just loneliness or the fact that she had no friends, or the fact that she had been shut up in this house for years. She had been shut up out of choice. She had no friends out of choice. Their choice probably.

She had no friends because she was arrogant, and I believed she was arrogant and nasty because she was ill. Everyone in Cornwall had thought of her as such a helpful and caring person, if a little bossy. Yet I was beginning to think she was some kind of narcissist for her constant criticism of other people and her need to be right all the time. She was so desperate to prove that I was wrong that she would lie about something that everyone knew could not possible be true.

I wondered if it was some kind of insecurity, but why would it be?

This house was paid for and her name was on the deeds, according to what she had told me. It was huge and packed with antique furniture that was also packed with antique stuff that was possibly worth a fortune. She didn't have to work because she had a man who loved her and supported her and made sure she had everything she needed. She had nothing to be insecure about; apart from the fact that she was horrible and no one liked her.

Whereas I was stumbling through life from one muddle to the next, leaving a trail of half written stories and strange diary entries as I struggled to make sense of the world. And there I sat; locked up in Spain, with my van in Portugal without its engine and my need to be in England. I was sure she was going to ask me to leave at any moment even though I had nowhere to go and I could be arrested if I was found out of the village, or even out of the house without good reason.

So, no. I did not think she was this way because she was insecure. I believed she was this way because she was, quite simply, round the flipping twist.

It was the next day that I put my life – or at least my hair – in her hands.

One of the things I had forced into my small bag when I had left Portugal was a box of hair dye. My roots had already begun to show and I had thought it would be easier to sort out in Ruth and Stuart's bathroom than in a bucket in my van inside Raymond's garage. But since we had gone into lockdown I had not bothered. I had thought that I could do it a day or two before we were allowed out to mix with the general public again. But Ruth had other ideas.

"You need to get some of that grease off your hair," she informed me that morning.

"What grease?" I asked, quite insulted.

"It's thick with it, that's why you tie it up." She said.

"I tie it up because I'm hot, I only washed it yesterday." I struggled not to throttle her. I could smell her own hair from where I sat, yet there she was criticizing my clean hair!

"Your roots are almost to your pony tail."

"I know, it doesn't matter, I'll dye it before I leave."

"I'll do it for you now if you want."

I didn't want. In fact I was horrified at the thought of her being let loose on the long blond locks I spent so much time caring for.

But I was instructed to "Go and fetch the dye and sit in the patio," while she got her bag out.

I only had one box. I had wanted to look reasonable when I left and not while I was shut up with the modern version of Laurel and Hardy. But I did as I had been told and fetched the box and waited at the patio table. I thought that she couldn't really do too much harm as long as she didn't get the scissors out.

And so I sat in the sun and tried to stay calm while she plastered the dye over my head and face, and my shoulders, and the back of the chair, and one of the cats. But I saw no sign of the scissors. When she had finished she went back into the house and I found a cloth to wipe the stuff off the floor tiles before it did any damage and watched the cat throw up after attempting to clean itself. Twenty minutes later I went into the downstairs bathroom and turned on the shower. I undressed, folded my clothes twice, cut my toenails and looked in the mirror to check my eyebrows for strays while I waited for the cold to run from the pipe and the hot to finally reach the shower head.

When I got out of the shower and towel dried my hair I didn't really have the courage to look in the mirror. So I got dressed first and then took a deep breath and looked.

No difference. Well, not on my left side anyway. My right side didn't look too bad; most of the grey was covered, and my hair is naturally several shades darker at the back anyway. But my left side looked just the same as before, with grey roots a couple of inches long and no evidence that any kind of dye had been anywhere near them. I consoled myself with the thought that light grey to blond on one side wasn't quite as bad as Ruth's chestnut front to steel grey back.

"Oh that's much better" she said, "You really should have it done properly more often."

"Humm, thanks. I should." I told her

Oh gods, I had been dying my own hair roughly every six weeks for more than 40 years and I had never looked this bad!

I tried to console myself by changing my nail varnish, but as soon as I had I collected the things I needed and put them on the patio table, I was taking them back to my room again. Ruth had been horrified at the thought of my using nail varnish remover outside. "That stuff is fucking inflammable," she yelled, "It's too hot out here for inflammable liquids, get it inside at once." I did so. There really was absolutely no point in my trying to explain how hot it really need to be to ignite anything, and I really didn't fancy one of her lectures at that point.

The world continued to turn. Some people were praising the NHS and others were still claiming it was all a hoax. I asked again how the all governments of the world had managed to get together to organize this hoax and a friend in Norfolk suggested that maybe he should ask his undertaker son to dig up some of the bodies he had buried and tell them they couldn't have died because there was no virus. And I felt miserable because my ferry left Calais for Dover and I was still stuck in Spain. It was also the anniversary of the day my beloved little dog had crossed the Rainbow Bridge, and as this all came shortly after my deceased son's birthday I felt very low.
So I spoke to some people from home.

One was a much loved friend, who was known to be partial to sniffing things he shouldn't. He told me that there was no virus, no one he knew had been ill and no one had died, and I should just get on with my life as normal. He told me he was still working.
"How is scaffolding considered essential?" I asked.
"Everything is essential," he said, "It's essential that I go to work because otherwise I'd starve."

I laughed. "More likely it's essential because you are incapable of sitting still," I said. In the six years I had known this man I had never seen him sit down for more than three minutes, even when we had gone out to eat. He is the only person I have ever had to ask "Will you please sit still?" while he was driving.

The other was a lovely lady I had met while working on the markets. She was the first person I knew to have Covid. She and her husband had both had a mild dose of the virus and were finding it hard to recover. They had been told it would be a long time before they would feel 100% again, if ever.

I also spoke to one of my brothers and learned that he was self isolating. There was no need for him to self isolate; he was just happier being alone and hoped he would never have to go back to work. He said his garden was looking lovely and he had painted the shed.

Then Ruth started dropping hints by telling me that there were fights all over Europe and I could get back to Portugal easily. Apparently Stuart could track them on his phone. So I asked him.

"Have you ever heard of Wizz airlines?" he asked. I said I hadn't and he told me neither had he but they were flying from London to Lisbon daily. "So not a lot of good to you then," he said. While I was still wondering how he knew what they were doing if he had never heard of them he got out his phone. We both checked the internet for flights and found nothing that was not going from one major city to another with 'essential only' passengers. But Stuart knew there were lots of flights because he had an app of some sort that allowed him to track all flights all over the world. He got out his phone and showed me that one was about to land in Lisbon within a few minutes. It had come from London and he told me when it had left, how high it was flying and at what speed, what type of plane it was and how many engines it had, but he ignored me when I asked the pilots name and what colour underpants he had on. Having seen this he told me that they do fly all over Europe all the time. Maybe not as often as usual, but they were still up there. I asked one more question about this flight.
"What is it carrying?"
He looked a question at me.
"It might not be a passenger plane, it might be cargo." I said. Realization dawned and he quietly put his phone away. He shrugged, "Didn't think of that," he said.
Later I heard them arguing about me with Ruth saying that I could get a flight from Madrid to Lisbon and Stuart asking how the hell I was going to get to Madrid and even if I could get to Lisbon how the hell was I going to get across the country to where I needed to be.
"Anyway, she doesn't have residency, so they won't let her in." he said.
That was something I hadn't thought of, but of course he was right. Portugal was only letting people in if they had a home there. And I didn't.
"Well she can go to London, then," announced Ruth.

"And go where?" Stuart spoke my thoughts. "She doesn't even have a home to go to there right now, does she? And what about her van? She can't just leave it. She's got to wait till she can get back to Portugal." I was pleased to hear that he spoke calmly, that he didn't seem angry at the thought of my staying. Ruth was, that was clear, but Stuart seemed to be on my side. Or at least he had enough brain power to realize that there was nothing I could do. I didn't blame them; this was their home and they were used to being alone there. I had only been planning on staying for two weeks, and here I was, two months later with no hope of leaving in sight.
But Ruth wasn't finished yet.

The next morning I knew I was in trouble when I found her in the Breakfast/dining room when I got up. She waited until I had my coffee but my bum was still a couple of inches from the chair when she asked, "What have you done about leaving?"
"What can I do?" I asked
"You've got to find a way to get back to Portugal. I don't know how you are going to do that because you never talk to me….." and on she went, and on and on, about how she doesn't know what I'm doing, and I can't stay here forever, and I never tell her what my plans are. I tried to speak several times but she wouldn't shut up long enough to listen. So I walked away.
"Get back here! Don't you walk away from me," she shouted. I wanted to give my usual response to that; I wanted to say 'Why not, who the hell are you? My mother?' but I didn't. I just went back and said "What's the point if you don't listen to me."
"Go on then…" she demanded.

"What do you want me to do? There are no buses, no trains, no planes and I can't get over the border. I can leave this house if you want me to but I will have to name you if I get arrested for breaking lockdown rules." And then I walked away, stunned that I had been able to say all that without interruption. As I walked towards my room at the front of the house I saw Stuart coming down the stairs and heading for where Ruth sat. He did not look happy.

I went back to my room and sat and thought. But I really had no choice. I wanted to leave as much as she wanted me gone, but I had nowhere to go and no way to get there. There were plenty of abandoned buildings I could move into and it wouldn't be the first time I had done that, but I didn't even have a sleeping bag, let alone something to cook on. If she really wanted me to leave I would have no choice but to walk down to the village council office and tell them why I had nowhere to go. But, thanks to Stuart, I didn't need to.

I left it about two hours before I went back to where they were still sitting and I told them that I had contacted the embassy, the border control, the airline I came with, the train company and the mechanic. In fact I had done none of this, not that morning anyway. I had contacted them all about a month previously and the embassy even had me down as being in a vulnerable situation, and were contacting me via email once a week to check that I was still OK. I toyed with the idea of telling them when I had really done all this, but felt that it might cause another problem. It would mean that Ruth wasn't really in control of what I did and I had worked out by then that this was actually what she needed. To be in control. So I let them both think that I had only done all this because Ruth wanted something done.

I was pleased to find that they both sat and listened to me, Ruth looking at her phone and Stuart looking at Ruth.

Then he said, "You can't leave, that would be silly. You have nowhere to go and it's not legal anyway. You will have to stay here until you can get back to Portugal because you can't even go to England, can you?"
"No." I said.
"You can't go to England because you have nowhere to go to and you can't go to Portugal because they won't let you. You don't really exist anywhere, do you?"
"No." I said.
"Then we will all just have to get along with each other for a bit longer."
Ruth was nice to me for the rest of the day.
But I was told, quite clearly, to mind my own business when it came to Thomas.

Thomas had continued to follow me around but had started acting a little odd at times. He no longer wanted to play and started sitting under the table by my door instead of on top of it. He would let me go to him and make a fuss of him, but he no longer came running to greet me. And he stopped eating any ham I might sneak to the floor for him. A couple of times I let him into my room and we sat on the bed together as I stroked him. But then he stopped even trying. When I did see him, which wasn't very often, he just looked sad. I knew there was something wrong, but I was ignored. I tried telling Ruth something wasn't right, but she insisted I was wrong. She said he was her cat and I didn't know him, nor did I know anything about cats at all. She waved me away with her hand and told me to mind my own business.

****

There was an announcement that someone in the village had died. Ruth pulled her vape thing out from between her breasts, took a puff and then told me that she didn't know why he had died and she didn't know why the announcement hadn't told us. Stuart pointed out that we had been told just yesterday that no cases of Covid had been reported in the village so it could have just been old age. But she wasn't having that, she needed to know. So while I sat and tried to find out what Jack Reacher was up to in a village called Hope, I had to try not to listen to what she and Stuart were saying. It didn't work, and as Reacher drove into a place called Despair I gave up and listened.

Stuart translated the announcement almost word for word; it had just said that a man had died. Not who he was, or how old he was, or what he died of.

"Well, if he died at home no one will ever know," said Ruth.

"What?" Stuart was voicing my thoughts again, which isn't often a good idea.

"If he died at home no one will ever know what he died of."

"Well, *we* won't know, but *we* don't need to."

"No one will know," her voice was rising, "Not if he died at home."

"Maybe he was ill, maybe he had cancer, maybe someone was with him." He looked directly at her and added, "Maybe someone killed him."

"Yes, but now he's dead no one will know why he died."

Keeping my head still I continued to look over the top of my glasses at Stuart. His face was a picture of confusion.

"If they don't know they can find out," he said.

"How the fuck can they find out?" she was annoyed now, raising her voice.

"They'll do a fucking post mortem," he was raising his voice to match hers, it must have been reverberating off the garden walls and right around the entire village.

"They can't do a fucking post mortem because he died at home and they only do that in hospitals!"

"They'll take him to fucking hospital, or the morgue, or fucking somewhere else and do it."

"Don't be so fucking stupid, you don't know what you're talking about."

It was at this point that I managed to slide out of the garden and back into the house without being noticed because they were both staring at each other and shouting. Knowing that their voices would be echoing off walls all around the village I just hoped the dead man's poor family didn't understand English.

Half an hour later they were arguing again. Something about the disinfectant we have to use to spray over the cat pee. Stuart insisted that he had left it somewhere downstairs and Ruth insisted it was upstairs. While he shuffled about searching the stable and the back room she followed him telling him that he should fucking open his eyes and look for it, and I stood in the kitchen looking at it. I decided that it was probably safer for me to simply go and sit in the garden. I sometimes thought I didn't really need to go out of the house to walk back and forth along the road. I got plenty of exercise walking around the house avoiding Ruth.

****

Ruth decided she was on a diet and I'm glad she told me because I would never have guessed judging by the amount of ready meals and pizza's she was eating. Not to mention the huge crusty bread rolls filled with cheese that she polished off every lunchtime. Because of her diet we had to go shopping every six days but I decided not to ask how this made a difference, I simply got in the car when I was told to. And one day this was actually quite funny.

The car had a sliver film over the windows at the back so although we could see out no one could see in. Ruth and I would sit in the back for our trips to the next village and the two small supermarkets so it looked like Stuart was alone in the car. On this particular day Stuart spotted a police car sitting by the roundabout and he mentioned it.
"Oh no!" said Ruth, "There's too many of us in here," and she immediately hunkered down to hide. I moved my head just enough to catch the grin on Stuarts face in the rear view mirror and then moved it back again. We got around the roundabout and Ruth sat upright again. But just as she did so Stuart said, "On no, he's following us." And she flung herself down again.
"He's still there," he said after about a minute.
I turned around to look out of the rear window and saw the police car in the distance. He wasn't actually following us; he just happened to be there, had probably just stopped by the roundabout to have a break or make a phone call and was now on his way again. But Ruth was still hugging her knees so I said, "Oh, yes, he's there, coming up closer now."
"Don't worry," said Stuart, "I'll lose him on the bend." And he flung the car around a corner faster than necessary and I put my hand on the door to steady myself.
"Oh my God!" muttered a worried Ruth.
I turned around again and saw that the police car had not followed us around the corner.
"Nice one Stuart, you've lost him." I said.
Ruth sat upright and looked around at me. "You should have got down!" she said. Even when she saw that I was laughing she didn't understand. "I'm not fucking paying any 600 euro fine for you!" she told me.

****

I began to miss Thomas. He just wasn't around as much as he had been and I hardly saw him now. But whenever I mentioned it to Ruth she dismissed it by saying that he's not my cat or that I didn't know what I was talking about. But I was sure there was something bothering him. And I was concerned for the female and her kittens next door as well. I had not been allowed to go when Ruth went to feed them and I was glad because the house smelled of damp and the yard of pee and poo. But Ruth had said she had not heard or seen anything of the kittens although she was certain they would be fine. But then the female started crying as if she were in heat again. "She sounds like Gail used to." I said, "And look at him." I pointed to Ginger who had given up trying to get out of the back garden and was currently sitting in the patio looking up at the top of the wall in the direction of the sound. "I think she's calling him and he wants to answer but he can't get there."
"Oh don't be stupid," Ruth said, "She's got kittens, cats don't come into season when they have kittens. And she not calling him, cats don't communicate with each other."
"I think they do," I said.
"They don't, and anyway, Nuts is being fixed so it won't matter then."
I had no idea what had transpired between Stuart and Ruth and the owner of the cats, and I had no intention of asking, but it was now clear the Ginger was to be neutered and Stuart was paying for the operation. I also had no idea why Ruth thought that would make the cat next door safe. She and I had sat in the garden and watched another tom run along the roof tops and drop down into next doors yard. I had said something like, "Maybe that will stop her crying," but Ruth had said nothing and I had wondered if she had understood what I meant.

Although Ginger was now part of the family he was not allowed in the main part of the house at night. They allowed him to sleep either on a specially made bed under the terrace in the garden or on a blanket on a sofa in the back room. But they prevented him from coming into the main part of the house by sealing off the cat flap from the back room to the kitchen. They even put the rubbish bin in front of it, blocking its movement, in case the clip fails. But one morning Ruth got up early to find Ginger asleep on the sofa in the living room. She told me that he had obviously sprayed everywhere because she could smell it and I wondered how she could tell the difference as the house usually smelled of cat pee anyway, although, of course, I said nothing. Then she told me that she was confused. I knew that her mind was permanently confused, but again, I said nothing. She seemed to think I should know how Ginger got into the house because she knew that she had put him out the previous night and she knew that Stuart would not come down in the middle of the night to let him in. "So I'm confused," she said, staring straight at me accusingly, "I don't know how he got in."
I shook my head, "I'm sorry, I have no idea," I said truthfully, and I watched as her lips tightened almost to the point of disappearing. She didn't release them for some time and she and I even sat in the garden together in total silence while I waited for the explosion as she sat ramrod straight with a face like thunder. I didn't have to wait for long because Stuart soon appeared and was pounced on the minute he stepped through the door.
"Nuts was in the house all night and he sprayed and I don't understand how he got in," she said loudly while looking directly at me. Stuart eased himself into a chair and said, quite calmly, "The patio door was open."
"The patio doors are always open, he was in the house." She said.

"I know." Said Stuart, "I mean the other door, the one to the living room." He then explained that he had heard a commotion during the night and had come down to find Ginger and Linda hissing at each other and he had seen that the door was open. Ruth wanted to know why he hadn't put the cat out and he explained that it had been four o'clock in the morning and he hadn't felt like chasing a cat around the house at that time. He said that he could, of course, have woken her up to help him but he hadn't thought that would be a good idea.
Ruth had assumed that I had let the cat in for some reason but had been proved wrong. She hardly spoke to me for the rest of the day. In fact she hardly spoke to Stuart either. Instead she spent most of the day in the breakfast/dining room, sitting at the table with her laptop, searching the internet for something unknown. I spent a pleasant day sitting in the garden reading or listening to one of Stuarts stories from his childhood.

Ruth started getting up early and I would often find her at the table before I even had my first coffee. One such morning the first thing she said as I entered the room was "Gail was stuck outside all night." As Gail was a cat and the garden was enclosed I had no idea that this was a problem. But apparently it was. The bin was put in front of the cat flap to stop Ginger getting in, and Ruth now told me that the bin had been moved so Gail had got out, but couldn't get in again.
I thought about that for a bit before asking, "But why not, if the bin had been moved."
"Because the cat flap only works one way." I thought that this must mean that all the cats could get out but not get in again, so I wondered why the bin had been there in the first place, but I thought it best not to ask.
"I don't know why the bin was moved." Ruth said.
"Neither do I," I replied, and we sat in stony silence until Stuart came in.

It turned out that he had come down to the bathroom in the middle of the night and noticed Gail in the patio, knowing her only way back inside was through the cat flap he had moved the bin. The fact that she hadn't wanted to come back in was not his fault. He then got a telling off for not knowing that the cat flap was locked from that side only and I watched him close his eyes. I wondered if that was desperation or the beginnings of a possible explosion.

Then, "But why was she out there in the first place?" demanded Ruth.

"Because you didn't check where she was last night and locked her out there."

Silence.

"You locked up last night," Stuart said, and the matter was dropped.

Ruth spent another day at her laptop and I spent another pleasant day with my book.

*****

We drifted into May and the rules changed. Finally we were allowed out of the house to exercise. But only for an hour a day and we had to stay within a kilometer of the house.

I asked Stuart and Ruth if they wanted to come for a walk but Stuart didn't feel good and Ruth didn't understand why anyone would want to go for a walk just for the sake of it. That was a dumb thing to do and a waste of time, and she returned to searching the internet for things she didn't want or need and Stuart was going to have to pay for. I set off in the direction of the river and spent a very pleasant couple of hours wandering about by its banks and sitting in the shade with my toes in the water and reading another Jack Reacher story. Over the next few weeks I spent a lot of time sitting by that river, it was a little bit of heaven in a messed up world and when I sat there listening to the sweet tones of Israel Kamakawiwo'ole singing from my phone I could almost believe I really was in paradise.

But that first day I got back to the house to some upsetting news.

Ruth had been to feed the cats next door and had seen the mother cat for the first time. She now admitted that she had not seen her before, but had just picked up the empty food bowl and left the full one. However, that morning the mother cat had been sitting on the step to one of the back rooms and had not moved when Ruth walked towards her. Instead she had just cried. Ruth had stepped right passed her and gone to look for the kittens with no resistance from her. She had found one of the kittens and now asked me to go next door with her and fetch it so she could bury it. Stuart was against the idea and said we should leave it there, but I agreed with Ruth so he was outnumbered and we went. Ruth stood at the foot of the steps while I went up and found the dead kitten behind some building materials. Using a broom I swept it closer to me and then put my hand inside a plastic bag to pick it up. Once I had it tied up in the bag I dropped it down to Ruth and climbed over the building stuff to look further. And there I found another dead kitten. This one must had died several weeks before as it was a lot smaller and mostly rotted away. It was little more than a blob of fur, covered in maggots, but there defiantly was at least one leg so I was sure it was the other kitten. I left it there. As I climbed back I saw mother cat, just sitting and watching me. I think she knew what I was doing. She knew I had found both her babies and we both knew that they had gone. I gently sat down and she and I looked at each other for a while. I hoped that she would realize that I did understand her pain. I know what it is like watch your own baby die, but this poor cat had done it twice. I wanted to take away her pain; I wanted to tell her that everything was going to be OK and that she was loved. I wanted to pick her up and take her away and look after her. But I had no choice but to leave her there in that shithole. I really hoped she somehow understood that there really was nothing I could do.

For the next six weeks I had to listen to her cry and I believe she was crying with loneliness. Eventually she learned to climb up onto the roof just as the other two cats had done before her, but I never saw her free. Instead she would sit on the top of the wall and look down into the patio at her brother and the other cats and know that she couldn't join them. It almost broke my heart and I kept hinting that she should be allowed to join Ginger and the others.

But Ruth was adamant it was not going to happen. I tried suggesting that we go back to the house and put a plank of wood up so she could at least get out of the garden, but I was informed that then she would become a feral cat and feral cats don't live very long. I felt it would be better to have a short life than a long and lonely one. I was reminded that I knew nothing about cats and I should mind my own business. Maybe that was my fault; maybe I should have told Ruth that I have owned several cats and they have all lived to be quite old. But I never really had the chance and it would only have made the situation worse. I had to remind myself that I wasn't speaking to a normal person; I was speaking to someone with a brain defect. I had to accept that she had five cats and she wasn't going to have another.

All too soon she was back to only having four, but she still refused to allow this poor mother cat to have any attention.

CHAPTER SEVEN

"Where's Thomas?" I asked Stuart.
"Upstairs, under my bed." He said.

I asked if he was OK and mentioned that I hadn't actually seen him for several days. Stuart told me that he had been taking his food upstairs for him, but that he hadn't really eaten very much. "Is there a litter tray up there?" I asked, because I had seen no evidence of anything being brought down.

"I'll take one up today." He said.

I was stunned. This poor cat hadn't been downstairs for several days, which meant that he was either doing what he had to do on the carpet, or he wasn't doing it. A couple of days later Stuart told me that he hadn't emptied the tray because there was nothing to empty, but he didn't seem to be concerned.

"I think you need to take him to the vet when you take Ginger," I said.

But Stuart didn't think so. "He'll be fine in a day or so," he said.

"There's nothing wrong with him," came a bossy voice from the doorway. "He's just sulking because Nuts is here. Once Nuts has his nuts off Thomas will be fine." I didn't agree, but looking at her face I knew the conversation was over.

Ginger couldn't go to the vets straight away because he was ill. His eyes were watering and then becoming crusty and his nose was running. He would also sneeze. I had never seen that in a cat before and I asked what was wrong. Stuart said that he hoped it was just a cold and not cat flu because cat flu was dangerous. But he and Ruth had agreed that the cat needed to have clear airways before an operation. And I agreed with that.

Another couple of days and I spoke to Stuart again. This time he told me he would take Thomas to the vet at the end of the month when he got paid. I offered to lend him the money but Stuart didn't want that. "Will you let me pay for it then?" I asked.

No, he wouldn't, but he was very quiet about it. "I can't see him being that ill, please, let me pay." But the answer was no. I never really knew if that was pride or fear of upsetting Ruth, or if Stuart really did believe the cat would be fine once Ginger had stopped spraying everywhere.

Whenever I mentioned Thomas to Ruth she told me I didn't know what I was talking about. My saying that I thought he might be constipated and that can be dangerous in a cat was laughed at as stupid. Had we not been in lockdown I would have taken the cat to the vet myself. But, as it was, the vet was closed and only able to perform emergency treatment booked over the phone, and I didn't even know where the vet was. The vet had agreed to spade Gail and neuter Ginger and both these operations had to be paid for on the credit card, so I didn't understand why Thomas couldn't be seen for illness. I felt his case was more important than having Ginger's bits removed.

After about a week Stuart brought Thomas downstairs to join the others at breakfast time. The others ignored him. Poor Thomas simply sat where he had been put and looked longingly at the food. But he didn't touch it. Stuart then picked him up again and took him out to the garden, hoping he would play with the others when they came out. But he didn't. He simply sat where he had been put and watched. And cried.

I went to stroke him but he just looked at me and cried. "You're hurting him," snapped Ruth. I knew I wasn't, I hadn't even touched him. Thomas was trying to tell us he was in pain, but I said nothing. I just went to a chair and sat down. I looked at Stuart and saw that he looked utterly miserable. This so called man, who had quietly taken his common law wife in hand to defend me, would not defend his cat. I never understood why he wouldn't, but I know it broke his heart.

As we sat there, chatting and watching four of the five cats playing in the sun, my suggestion that Thomas was in pain was ignored and Thomas quietly walked away and hid. I found him a few minutes later, hiding inside a flower pot in the patio. He looked up at me and cried. I took a photo of him because there was nothing else I could do, and even in that photo I can see he is asking for help. He is trying to make someone understand that he hurts and he needs help. But he didn't get it until it was too late.

Even though Ruth had not been alone with Thomas that day, even though the three of us had been in the garden and I alone had found him in the flower pot and even though I had watched as Thomas struggled out of the pot, walked slowly across to the stairs and struggled out of my sight, apparently Ruth had checked him over without either Stuart or myself knowing. Because the next day she announced that she had looked in his mouth and seen that his gums were white. This, she said, was a sign that the cat was anemic. I didn't understand right then why she had waited until that point to tell us what she had done the day before, but I did later. Ruth also claimed that Stuart was wrong and Ginger didn't have cat flu because he didn't have 'the shits' and diarrhea was a sure sign cat flu. She hadn't mentioned this before so I was actually quite pleased to hear it now. Not only was she admitting that Thomas might be ill, but it seemed as if she had maybe Googled cat flu because she was concerned about the wellbeing of another living creature other than herself. But I was wrong.

Ruth spent a lot of time watching English TV on her Ipad thing. (My apologies, I have no idea what these things are really called and I don't actually care enough to find out). She had once told me that she had been watching Jo Brand and I had said, "Oh I like her, she's very funny" to be met with a look so vacant I wondered if she might have been one of Jo's original patients.

"It's a programme about cats," she had said. So, later on this particular day I asked what this programme was called to see if I could find it and watch it. I was informed that I wouldn't be able to find it and I would have to let her set it up on Catch-up (whatever that was) for me. So that is what she did, and I donned my earphones and sat at the table to watch Jo Brand rescue dozens of cats from one tiny apartment. And there I found why Ruth had waited almost 24 hours to say that she had looked into the cat's mouth, and I learned that she hadn't cared enough to Google anything.
Because Jo Brand had told her.
Some of the cats that Jo helped to rescue had cat flu and the vet explained the symptoms, mentioning the diarrhea. Not only that, but later it was mentioned that another cat was anemic and this was shown by the fact that its gums were white. I could hardly believe that Ruth was daft enough to let me watch this just hours after claiming to know those things herself. She hadn't mentioned anything about cat flu and diarrhea a few days before when we had all be talking about Ginger's condition. She had only mentioned it after she had watched this show. And a few hours later she allowed me to watch the same show.
And she claims I am stupid!

Soon enough Ginger recovered from his cold and went to have his jewels removed. But Thomas didn't even get a check up because Ruth wasn't convinced he was ill. She was still sure he would be fine once he realized that Ginger was no longer a full tom. Stuart kept quiet and I knew there was no point in my talking to him. I had offered to pay, I had offered to lend the money, I had almost begged him to take the cat to the vet but nothing had worked, Stuart still had to think what Ruth told him to think. It wasn't until Ginger went back for a post op check up that Thomas finally went as well. Ruth still wasn't sure he needed a vet because he was only anemic, but by now Stuart was finally losing patience. They had no problem putting Thomas in his box for the trip, he cried, but he didn't bother to struggle, the poor cat could hardly move. His eyes met mine just before the lid was shut and I tried to look sympathetic, wanting him to know that I cared.

Both cats came back with antibiotics, Ginger for a slowly healing wound and Thomas for stomach ache. Stuart was quite tactful in telling Ruth that he had mentioned white gums and the vet had checked but found everything OK, so Ruth wasn't actually told she had been wrong. He then said that Thomas had been given an injection to 'clear him out' so I wasn't actually being told that I had been right about him being constipated. He went on to say that if Thomas wasn't any better in the morning he was to go in for an operation. Stuart never actually said what that operation was and Ruth didn't ask. I didn't need to ask because I had Googled it and found that I had been right. Constipation in a cat was dangerous and if it cannot be cleared an operation would be needed. I don't know why Ruth didn't ask. Maybe she did when I wasn't around, maybe she just didn't really care.

Thomas never got that operation.

Later that night, as the three of us sat in the living room ignoring each other Thomas started to cry. Stuart went upstairs to fetch him and sat him on the foot stool by his feet. But the cat just cried. Stuart picked him up and sat him on his lap. But the cat just cried, and it was a heart rending cry of pain.
"I think he might need that operation right now." I suggested.
"He can go back to the vet in the morning." Ruth said.

May the gods forgive me; but I got up and walked away.

I knew what was happening and I knew it was already too late. There was nothing I could do. But I couldn't sit by and watch. I couldn't even listen. Had he been my cat I would have put him in the car and driven to the nearest vet to bang on the door for help. Actually no, had he been my cat he would not have been allowed to get into that condition in the first place. But he wasn't my cat and I had no control over what happened. Without the lockdown maybe things might have been different, maybe I would have snatched him and taken him to a vet two weeks ago. But he wasn't my cat, and we were in Lockdown, and I didn't even speak the language well enough to do anything.
So I walked away.
I went to my room and I sat on the bed and I cried. I rocked myself backwards and forwards and over and over again I muttered the words "I'm sorry, I'm so sorry." Because I had done nothing.
And Thomas cried like a frightened child.
And then he screamed.
And screamed.
It was the worst sound I have ever heard in my life. It was a scream of agony. Not like you hear in the movies, this was a sound so horrible it cannot be described.
An hour later it stopped. The house fell silent, and I cried myself to sleep like a child.

The following day Thomas was buried in the garden while I went back to the river to find my own way of letting him go. Mental condition or not, I will never forgive Ruth for allowing that to happen. She allowed that poor creature to die, screaming in agony, because she was determined to always be right. And Stuart didn't have the balls to stand up to her until it was too late.

CHAPTER EIGHT

I decided I needed to know.
I needed to know if Ruth really was mentally deranged, or just nasty. Of course I couldn't exactly take her to a doctor and it's not considered polite to ask someone if they have ever been dropped on the head from a great height or if their parents were brother and sister, so I sat in my room and made a list of what I thought might be symptoms. It was a long list.
Then I Googled each symptom separately and the internet threw back all sorts of medical problems. One problem kept showing up again and again.
Covert Narcissist.
Reading the list of symptoms was like reading a description of Ruth. A person who appears to be a helpful and caring person, but really it's all done to only benefit themselves. To make themselves seem important. I thought of how Ruth had worked (paid) at the charity shop 'because she cared' and then how I had seen her leaving with huge bags that were nowhere in sight when she had arrived. I thought of the things I had seen in her house in Cornwall that I had previously seen donated to the shop. I thought of the way she claimed to be a huge cat lover yet would not listen to me when I said something was wrong with Thomas. She was only interested in proving that she knew more than I did.
Then I found 'Opinionated.'

Yes, defiantly. No one else was allowed to have an opinion at all because whatever Ruth said Ruth believed to be fact and if I didn't agree with her all hell would break lose. To attempt to tell Ruth she might be wrong was to sign my own death warrant.

Ruth was, I decided, an Opinionated, Covert Narcissist.

Stuart actually went up in my estimation that day. Because he had lived with Ruth, and coped with her, for some 38 years. I was seriously struggling after just two months! But I believe he needed her more than she needed him.

She needed him to pay for her very existence, and she needed him to boss about and be in charge of. But she would cope if he were to leave.

He needed her to tell him how to live. Although they argued a lot I think he thrived on it and I'm sure he would be totally lost without her. It's not uncommon for a man to need a bossy woman to obey; I just think that Ruth and Stuart's relationship went beyond the role play.

And that thought made me feel ill!

They had had separate bedrooms since I had known them, and Ruth would tell me how she couldn't bear to have him near her any more. I like the idea that these two were just house mates, maybe best friends. Because the thought of the two of them…….. No, sorry, I can't think of it!

But I felt a lot better knowing that I probably wasn't mistaken in my idea that she had a mental problem, and the more I read about this subject, the more I saw her on the pages.

She was an Opinionated Covert Narcissist. I was sure of it.

******

When Ruth appeared in the breakfast/dining room before 9am one morning I knew I was in trouble. Something was on her mind and she was determined to deal with it.

"You on that Facebook again?" she tried to sound friendly.

"No, I'm writing an email."

"You need to get a life," said the woman who doesn't leave her own house. Regardless of what I had actually said she had heard me say 'Why yes, of course, I am wasting time on Facebook again'.

I finished writing and tapped Send as she sat down next to me.

"You must have a lot of friends," she said sarcastically.

I nodded. "I do." I said.

"But you don't really know them all do you? Not really, they are just Facebook friends."

I took a deep breath; she was trying to carry on where Stuart had left off.

"Apart from a few cousins in Australia and New Zealand, I have met every single one of them, mostly before Facebook even existed." But I said it quietly and calmly, needing to get my point across without causing a row.

"Even that one in Hong Kong?" she asked.

"I don't know anyone in Hong Kong."

"Well, Japan, or wherever it is."

"There's James in Thailand and Claude in Vietnam, but I don't know anyone in………"

"How do you know them then?"

"I worked with James in Devon and with Claude in Israel."

She hissed like a pissed off cat, "Israel!" It's not often you hear one word said with such venom. "So he's from there, is he?"

"No, Claude is American; I just met him in Israel. He lives in Vietnam now."

"And how did you meet him there?"

"We worked together, with about 26 other people from all over the world."

"Doing what?"

"We all worked for the Department of Antiquities," Yes, I was getting a bit fed up by this time but my very basic, but honest, description of my time on the Hazan Dig at Moshav Amatzia had the desired effect. Ruth was quiet as she tried to find a way of pretending she knew what Antiquities meant. Eventually I explained.

"It's archeology."

"You're not an archeol…..ology thing, person!"

"No, none of us were, and none of us are. Except one. He wasn't but he is now and he's Israeli anyway. He's quite high up on the Antiquities ladder. Does a lot of writing about it. But you won't have heard of him; he writes in Hebrew." As she attempted to digest this I stood and added. "You know, I haven't heard from him in a while, maybe I should send him an email and see how the virus is disrupting the history of his part of the world." Using her own way of ending a conversation, I left the room.

That day I decided to walk along a road I didn't know. I took my phone so I had my map to get back and it was nice to just wander about getting lost. Ruth had previously told me that there was no way to get over the railway line at the top of the village, but that day I found two crossings. And several places where people had created crossings by just walking over the line so many times. I was meant to stay within a kilometer of the house, but I saw absolutely no one so I assumed that no one saw me. I found olive groves, and orange groves and lemon groves; I found small streams and tiny tracks that my map insisted were roads. I spotted tiny houses tucked away behind shrubs and trees and, of course, the obligatory bath tub in a field. I didn't stay out too long because it was getting hot, but I estimated that I had walked about 7 kilometers by the time I got back to the house.

Ruth asked me where I had been.

As I tried to explain I saw her eyes widen as she learned that I had got over the railway line after all. But then they glazed over and I knew she had no idea where I had been or what I was describing. When I had finished I left her, still in the same seat she had been in during the earlier conversation, and still in her dressing gown, and went to put the kettle on. Stuart was in the kitchen. As I spooned coffee into my mug he stood beside me and quietly said. "If you take her to the end of the road and spin her round, she won't be able to find her way back here." Then he opened a draw, moved some utensils around inside, and pulled out a bag of chocolate. We had one each, it was getting soft in the heat, and he put it back in its hiding place.

As it was getting hot I was told to keep the window in my room closed at all times. Stuart apologized for not having any net for it. He did try to get one but the DIY shops were not considered essential and were therefore closed. He told me that the mosquitoes would get in and I would be eaten alive. I learned that keeping the shutters closed during the heat of the day kept the room cool, but at night it was stifling so I had to have them open. The first hot night I wore leggings, socks and a long sleeved t-shirt and slept on top of the bed. I did not get bitten but I decided to buy some repellant so I could actually sleep without so many clothes on. The pharmacist sold me something to spray on every night before going to bed and this worked a treat. I also bought a special candle that was meant to ward of the little blood sucking bastards.
But I still got bitten a couple of times and once I was sure it was while I was in bed, under the cover. I turned to Google to find out if a mosquito could have survived in my bed for several hours and then bitten me once I got in. It couldn't. Then I looked at a photo of a mosquito bite; and I looked at the ones on my legs. They were different.

The next night I smothered myself in the repellant, but I still got bitten while in bed, or so I thought. I told Stuart and Ruth about it but Ruth was adamant that I was wrong. Stuart explained that I was probably being bitten before I got into bed but wasn't feeling it until later. That made a bit of sense so I started smothering myself in the repellant all day as well as at night. But I still got bitten.
Then I went back to the pharmacist and explained what had been happening and she asked what the bites looked like.
"They are just smooth lumps," I said, and I showed her the ones on my arm.
"This is not mosquito bite," she said, confirming what Google had told me.
So, I bought a different type of insect repellant and I sprayed my bed with it before I got in. I continued to cover myself in the mosquito repellant.
Then I had an idea.
I tried it out.

I slept a couple of nights without spraying the bed and all was fine. But the sheets had been on it for almost a week. Then I changed the sheets.
No longer being allowed to keep them in my room I had to ask each week for clean ones which Ruth fetched from her huge cupboard upstairs. She had shown it to me once and I had wondered why she had needed enough sheets to keep a hotel going for several months, but I had said nothing. Now she was bringing me different sheets each week, and they usually smelled as if they had been in the cupboard for years. That night I sprayed myself with the mosquito repellent as normal but did not spray the insect stuff onto the bed. And I got bitten almost as soon as I lay down.
I took a photo of the bites, sprayed the bed, waited half an hour and then got back in with my phone to do a search for what had attacked me.
Fleas.

I couldn't determine what type of fleas but they had to be cat. How or why they seemed to be in the linen cupboard was something I couldn't work out either. But something was being brought into my room with the clean sheets that Ruth gave me each week. Spraying the clean sheets with the bigger can of insect killer was killing them, but the thought of them even being there was horrible. I started vacuuming the bed each week as I wondered how it was all happening.

Then I noticed something.
Ruth was covered in bites. She scratched them and some of them bled and left scars. She always blamed mosquitoes and claimed that Stuart was lucky because they didn't like him. She would joke that they only liked sweet meat and not 'old stringy shit like Stuart.' Forcing myself to look, I saw that her legs and arms were a mess of bites, yet Stuart was clear. Assuming that the cats were regularly treated I looked at Ginger. He was the newest member of the household and I thought he would be the most likely to have fleas. But it turned out to be Linda I saw them on.
She had been sitting on the chair next to me in the patio, waiting for her ham when I saw one jump from her back onto the table. It was huge; I had never seen anything quite like it. I had a mental image of it waving a sword and shouting "Come on lads!" as it led a battalion of smaller fleas towards me. It defiantly appeared to be eyeing up my lunch. Thankfully F Company did not show up and General Ugly soon jumped away. If you've never actually watched one of those things jump, try to. It's quite amazing.
I mentioned the general to Ruth but, of course, she told me I was wrong. Her cats did not have fleas and neither did Ginger. There were no fleas on any of her cats, any of them! It was just a fly I had seen, it couldn't have been a flea, I don't know what I am talking about.

Well, I have never seen an oval shaped brown fly with a head that looks like a bird with its beak under its chin. And this thing had been so big I could almost see the hairs on its legs, but according to Ruth it must have been a fly.

A couple of days later I noticed Stuart in the kitchen with Linda pinned to the floor. As he let her go I saw that she had a wet spot on the back of her neck and Stuart had a small plastic bottle in his hand. "Two to go," he said.

I'd had a cat that had fleas once and I had been told to treat the house as well as the animal. But this house didn't get treated. Maybe it was because Stuart didn't know it needed to be, or maybe it was because he didn't want to admit to Ruth that he had even treated the cats, but the house did not get treated, and I still got bitten, usually as I was getting into bed. So I did a bit more reading about flea bites.

I learned that, just as Stuart had said about mosquito bites, flea bites don't always itch straight away, but often get worse as time goes on and can itch for up to a week. I thought that this might be what was happening to me. Once I started to itch I sprayed the offending spot with the alcohol that I had bought to spray my mask, and that seemed to stop the itch eventually. Ruth continued to scratch and parts of her legs looked like they had been bleeding.

Then I realized what was going on.

Stuart wasn't being bitten at all.

Ruth was covered in bites.

I only seemed to get them just before I got into bed, so I was getting bitten in the evenings. What did we all do in the evenings?

We sat in the living room.

Stuart sat on one sofa and Ruth sat on the other. I would either sit out in the patio or, occasionally, inside on the same sofa as Ruth. So I did a little experiment.

I spent the next three evenings in the patio and avoiding the sofa and I did not get bitten. Then I spent one evening inside, sitting on the sofa that Ruth used, with Maggie on my lap because I was in her spot, and I made myself stay there for two whole hours. Then I got up and then I started to itch. I had been bitten several times. It wasn't just Ruth who used this sofa, it was the cats as well, and I was now sure that their fleas had made a home in it.

That would explain why Stuart never got bitten, because even though the cats did sit on his sofa, their fleas (or whatever fleas they were) had made a home in the other one. It would explain why Ruth was constantly covered in bites and why I only ever got them in the evening.

Something was living in that sofa. Possibly the linen cupboard too, but defiantly the sofa.

I said nothing, but I made sure I never went near that sofa again, and I continued to spray my clean sheets, and the only bites I got were huge with hard spots in the middle when I forgot to cover myself with the mosquito repellant. I was never sure what kind of fleas or bugs were living in that piece of furniture, they could have been cat fleas or they could have been Ruth fleas, or a kind of bed bug. I'm not an expert, and I don't want to be, I don't want to even think about what they could have been!

CHAPTER NINE

About the middle of May I got an email from Raymond in Portugal. He had been allowed to go back to work. But he needed to let me know that he wouldn't be spending much time on my van because after two month off work he needed to work on cars that were quick and easy to fix, he needed an income. He then explained that he had the parts he needed for my van. So I took the hint and asked if he wanted me to pay for the parts he had already bought and he was grateful, he admitted that the money 'would be helpful' so I did a bank transfer to his company account for the cost of the parts and I said a silent prayer of thanks to whatever god or angel might exist that I was not having to pay any rent. I had, in fact, offered to pay something as rent but I had been told off for being offensive. And I had offered to pay for a gas bottle saying that I used a share of the fuel so felt it only fair that I paid for a share, but Ruth said I was being rude. I hadn't offered again. Now I was grateful I didn't have to pay. I should have been back at work by that point, my money wasn't going to last for much longer. I knew that Raymond still had bills to pay, both on the garage and his house, as well as to his ex wife for his son. But he hadn't worked for two months. I wasn't sure if Portugal would have any sort of furlough payment scheme in place so once I had paid what he had already spent I reminded him that I could not get into Portugal yet anyway, so I was in no hurry for my van.

Feeling the need to keep Stuart and Ruth updated as to what was going on I told them that Raymond was now allowed to go back to work so he would be getting on with my van quite soon.
"He should have had it ready by now," said Ruth and I guessed I was in for a hard morning. I didn't know then that I was actually in for a very hard day!
"No, he wasn't allowed to work for two months; he only started again this morning."
"Well, tell him to hurry up and get it done, you need it."

"But I don't," I said, "I can't go anywhere yet."
"Well, no, but tell him to hurry up, tell him you won't pay him till it's finished. This is daft, he's been messing about for too long." She waved a dismissive hand and turned back to her phone.
I kept quiet; there really was no point in my saying anything. But as I looked at her I couldn't help but wonder if there was some sort of poison I could sneak into her vape thing. People had been dying after vaping, hadn't they? It was said to be caused by cheap liquid from China, I thought. Maybe I could track some down from somewhere.
Walking from Valencia to Badajoz during a Lockdown looked quite appealing that day.

Then it got worse.
Ruth told me that her sister in England had been offered a grant for not being able to work. "That's good," I said, "Does it come from the government or her boss?"
I was then informed that Ruth's sister doesn't have a boss, that she is the boss, that it is her company, her restaurant, she and her husband own it, they paid for it, it's theirs, they are the bosses, they are not staff, they HAVE staff. Or at least, they had staff; they had to let them go because of being forced to close.
Excepting that I had been suitably put in my place I said, "Oh." Then "I wonder if I can claim, I'm self employed."
"You're not self employed!"
"Yes I am, have been for years."
"Don't be daft, you can't be self employed."

There then followed one of the many frustrating conversations that Ruth and I suffered as I tried to explain Self Employment to her. I tried to explain the difference between business owner and normal self employed. That her sister was a business owner and I was in and out of jobs; often doing two or thee at the same time; most of which were temporary, three of which I go back to year after year. This means that I work where I like for as long as I like and I can easily tell the tax man about it all. I didn't bother to explain that I could possibly get away without telling the tax man anything at all, but that I was too much of a wimp to do that, and besides, I needed to pay national Insurance for my own benefit.
"But your boss pays you money for the work you do." She said.
"Yes,"
"So you are not self employed, you work for the person who pays you."
"Yes, but there are lots of people who pay me, so it's easier to be self employed."
"No, it's illegal, you work for the person who pays you and they have to pay tax and national insurance for you. You are not self employed."
"But some of my jobs only last one or two days, so they don't have to pay……."
"Yes they fucking do!"
I tried another way…"Look, your sister runs a restaurant, right?"
"Yes,"
"So the people who eat there pay her, right?"
"Yes."
"So does she work for them? Do they pay her tax and national insurance?"
"Don't be fucking stupid!"
"But they pay her to serve them; they are paying her to work, in a sense."
"Yes, that's called being self employed, not what you do."

"It's the same kind of thing, but instead of people coming to me like they go to her restaurant, I go to them. Like a builder coming here and building a wall, you pay him, he works for you for that day, but you are not his boss, you don't pay his tax and National insr……"
"That's not the same thing, that's not being self employed, they are builders, they are not self employed, they work for a company."
"Not always."
"Yes, they do."
I decided not to bother telling her that I had been married to a self-employed builder for twenty years because I was beginning to accept that this was never going to work. No matter what I said she was not going to understand.
Then she said, "What you are doing is wrong, it's illegal."
I gave up, "Ok, maybe you are right, but the tax office seems to think it's perfectly ok so I guess I'll just carry on."
"It's wrong, you're wrong, you'll get caught, the tax office is………"
"I got my pension payment this morning, 2 Euros more than I thought, bonus eh?" Stuart had had enough and put a stop to the conversation.

But the day got worse.
After my lunch I only had one plate, one knife and one mug to wash, but there were two other plates on the unit. So I put some water in the sink and washed everything. But as I did so Ruth came and stuck her hand into the water. "I thought so," she said, "Its bloody cold. You need hot water to wash up in."
"It's only a couple of sandwich plates," I said.
"Look, you need hot water to kill the germs, now boil the kettle and do it properly."

As I waited for the kettle to boil I watched as Ginger sprayed the plates again and Gail walked across the kitchen work top, putting her foot on the plate that Ruth had left there and licking a tea cup of Stuarts. She walked a few more steps and then sat down to clean her bum.
I washed the tea cup, but left the plate.

But Ruth wasn't finished yet.
For dinner I had been cooking burgers under the grill and the fat had dripped out into the tray below. I asked where she wanted me to put the fat and was told 'down the sink.'
"Are you sure?" I asked, "It's the fat from the burgers."
"Yes, I'm fucking sure," she snapped, "It only came out of the burgers; it's not lard, is it?"
There was silence as I tried to take this in, then I said, quietly, "Ruth, that's what lard is, its animal fat."
"Oh fuck off!" and she dismissed me with a wave of her hand and stomped out of the room. I left it in the tray to go hard, then scraped it out and put it in the bin.
Later Ruth scratched a flea bite as she told me that I wouldn't have had any fat coming out of my burgers if I'd cooked them properly. Instead of bothering to explain that this is the exact reason why I grill them, I watched her scratch as I listened to her tell me how I should have fried them properly, in a frying pan, with oil, so that the fat didn't come out. Then the oil could have been put down the plug hole. And how my café training (another reference to my HND) was obviously crap if they didn't even teach me that.
I was quite proud that I managed not to be sick.

****

The lockdown rules were beginning to be lifted, one at a time. There were still no planes or trains or busses, and the Spanish/Portuguese border remained closed, but people were now allowed to travel within their home province. So I met Daan.

As I have said, this house was once part of a bigger house, and the bigger house also had its own bodega; a place where they made and stored wine. And it is still there, behind the wall of this garden. The wall was not there when Stuart and Ruth bought the house, but their land only goes half way to the bodega so, when they moved in, they went to the council and found out where their border was and built a wall. The Bodega had sat empty until Daan bought it the previous year.

All I knew at that point was that a Dutch couple had bought it and were turning it into a house. Ruth had told me that two of the pots that sat in her living room were presents from this Daan and his wife. Although no one had yet met the wife, they were sure she would be Dutch and not Thai, even though the couple owned houses in Thailand. I got the impression that they owned houses all over the place, and that they had sold one to pay for this one, and that the work had started just before Lockdown and was possibly going to restart soon.
Then Daan and his 'wife' paid a visit.
Maybe it's because I am totally accepting of these situations that I understood almost straight away, but Stuart and Ruth discussed it for the rest of the day. They decided that I might be right but I was probably wrong and they might have to wait until the couple moved in to be sure. But they really hadn't expected this as Daan had always talked about his wife.
Daan's wife is not Thai, is not Dutch.
Daan's wife is in fact Spanish.

I thought it was possibly a translation error and he simply didn't know the word Husband, but then I thought about Stuart and Ruth and decided that Daan might have been testing the water a bit before announcing that his 'wife' is actually another man.

As the two of them settled themselves into chairs in the patio I saw the looks between them and knew. Jose has a damaged hand and leg and Daan was clearly concerned as he sat down. A friend might have glanced over to check but a lover looks with more concern. Stuart seemed unconcerned and welcomed them both to his home while Ruth got out the best china and made a tray of tea. There were two cups and saucers on the tray, and her own mug of coffee. I waited as she poured tea for her two guests and then I got up and made tea for Stuart and coffee for myself.

Daan's English was very good and we all sat and chatted about all sorts of things until Daan mentioned the garden wall.

"We need to be sure everything is legal." He said.

"Of course it's legal," snapped Ruth.

"Yes, but my lawyer has told me something and I want to make sure we all agree so we don't have any problems in the future."

But Ruth had started talking before he had even finished. "Our lawyer isn't crooked, it's all legal." Having heard the story of how they took the money to pay for this house from the bank to the lawyers office in two plastic carrier bags, I wasn't so sure!

The two talked over each other for a while, Ruth being her usual bossy self and Daan trying to make her understand what his lawyer had told him. But she wouldn't listen.

I did. It seemed that Daan's lawyer had told him he could claim two meters of Ruth's garden and force them to move the wall back, but he didn't want to do that, he just wanted them all to go to the relevant office and sign papers to agree that the boundary was where the wall is now. He wanted to do this so there would be no problem in the future, if one of them died or wanted to sell.

Eventually I butted in with "Ruth, I think Daan is just trying to avoid a future problem, he actually wants to do you a favor."

"Yes," he said, "If I die, or sell, I don't want there to be a problem for you."

Stuart looked at Daan, then at me and then at Ruth. I don't think he had heard what either of them had said.

Ruth looked at me, then at Jose and then at Daan.

"He just wants you all to sign to agree that the wall is in the right place," I said.

"Of course it's in the right place," she snapped, still not grasping what was really going on.

But Stuart had heard enough and looked at Daan and asked, "So when do the builders start back to work on your place?" and the subject of the wall was dropped.

Later, as Daan and Jose were getting ready to leave Jose mentioned that they were going over to the bodega to see how things were getting on. So I took my chance.

"Do you mind if I'm really nosy?" I asked and both men laughed.

"You want to come and see it?" Daan asked.

"Yes please, if you don't mind." I said.

He smiled, "yes, of course, you can all come." He said.

Stuart and Ruth didn't really need to go. They had been many times. Somehow they had got hold of a key to the front door and have been going over there for one reason or another (mainly to bury cats I later discovered) for years. But they couldn't admit that.

Ruth took her time getting ready to leave the house and we all waited for her in the main room, where I saw Daan wrinkle his nose and look around. Jose pulled a face and I watched as his colour faded. He looked quite ill so I walked towards the main door – and away from the cat litter tray – as we talked, encouraging him to follow me. Eventually the three of us were standing by the door and that was when I realized that Gail had been there before us. I couldn't open the door for air because the cats would get out; they were always ready to shoot through that door like bullets as soon as there was a hint it was going to open. So the three of us shuffled back to the middle of the room again with Stuart looking on in confusion. Living permanently in that stink he could no longer smell it. Eventually Ruth reappeared and her overpowering perfume covered the stench of the cats and Daan, Jose and I all dived for to door at the same time. I watched Jose visibly relax and breathe deeply as he welcomed the hot, clean air into his lungs.

Off we all trooped, in a cloud of Ruth's Eau De China-cheap, past the side of the 17 bed roomed house to the end of the road, along its front and then back up its other side, to the building that backs onto the garden.

It's huge. I suspect way bigger than Stuart and Ruth's house, but it's almost all one room. They are having the floor made higher and the windows replaced, and then the main part of the house will be one giant room that Daan knows will be expensive to heat in the winter. The muddle of half rotten rooms to the side are to be made into kitchens, bathrooms, garages and bedrooms and the way the two men described it all I think it's going to be quite spectacular when it's finished.

"You must come and visit when it is all finished," said Jose.

"Oh, I'd love to," I replied, knowing I would never see it finished. Knowing that once I escaped this nightmare I was never likely to set foot in this village ever again. And wondering how I could warn them to change the locks without saying why.

*****

My morning walks started getting longer and longer. I admit that sometimes I just went to the river and sat with my feet in the water, but I also walked to the nearest villages. There was never anything to do when I got there, but it was nice to go and if I could walk back by a different route I would. By now I was doing roughly 12- 14 kilometers a day, and as I was able to walk in my crock flip flops my toe nails were growing back. I had done about the same distance each day earlier in the year, in Northern Spain but the weather wasn't as warm and I had worn closed in walking shoes. I'm not very good with shoes, my feet get hot and then swell and this causes me a lot of problems. But I have noticed that people can be quite rude if they see me in sandals in the winter time. I have even been told that it's a "sign of homelessness, of being dirty and slightly mental." And of course, if it's chilly and I wear toed socks with my flip-flops…...?
Yeah, I had to give that up!
But walking those distances with shoes on had damaged my toenails (and before you get on your high horse, my shoes are proper walking shoes that I was measured for, so they do fit) and two of them had turned black and then dropped off. Now they were growing in nicely, and I was much happier in my flip flops.

Ruth didn't think I was going very far at all; in fact she once told me that it wasn't possible to go very far by foot. Not at my age, and especially because I don't walk properly.
I had been quite insulted and after reminding her that she's only a year younger had asked what she meant. She had informed me that I don't walk properly. Apparently I 'plod' and that was because I have flat feet; I don't have any arches.

"Really?" was all I could think of to say because I actually have high arches and until I had my toes fused (due to arthritis) I often had to have special insole in my shoes to support them.

And when had she looked that closely at my feet?

"Yes," she continued, "You are defiantly flat footed, and heavy footed, you never learned to walk properly as a child. It's not possible for you to do any real distance."

I was quiet. It's not often I am speechless but on this occasion I really couldn't say anything because I didn't know where to start. I guess I could have started with the ballet classes I was forced to suffer as a child and where I was told I 'moved sublimely' and had been sure the teacher was swearing at me. Or I could have started with the various long distance walks of 50 to 60 miles that I had done for charity, or the miles I have walked a with a rucksack in my youth. But I didn't. I was just too stunned at her ignorance and rudeness.

The following day I walked to the nearest Mercadona and brought back some of the shops own brand of cat treats as proof. The nearest Mercadona to the house is seven kilometers away. Ruth had once insisted that it was seven miles away so I was expecting her to be quite impressed when I got back with the treats, but she wasn't. She just thanked me for the treats and reminded me that she usually buys the 'decent' ones.

I think the reason she wasn't impressed was because she has no concept of distance. She believed seven miles when it was seven kilometers, but if I'd walked seven yards she wouldn't have known how far that was either. She has no concept of height either and she kept insisting that she was four foot ten inches tall, yet she had to look down at me and I'm five feet tall!

Stuart took a different attitude to the way I walk. He said I caused a draft because I moved too fast. He also understood that I was finding it harder to walk as the days got hotter so he suggested I use his bike.

Stuart is something of a cycle enthusiast, and I don't mean just riding them. He would often acquire old broken down bikes and spend weeks taking them apart; cleaning and sanding, smoothing and painting, fixing and replacing and oiling. Eventually he would end up with what looked like a brand new bicycle which he would usually give away. He just did it as a hobby.

In his youth he had ridden way more miles than could be counted and had even raced. I think it was back in the 1960s that he had wanted to compete professionally but couldn't afford to buy the necessary bikes. I once heard a story that he had entered a race and won it only to be disqualified because his bicycle wasn't to the demanded standard. In other words, it wasn't a proper lightweight racing bike, but just a bog standard thing that he and his dad had put together from bits. So it was heavier and harder to ride. And he had still won the race.

One of his bikes now sat in the stable on some kind of stand that turned it into an exercise bike. It could be made easier or harder to ride by turning a dial on the handlebar. Stuart lowered the bike's seat and explained to me how it worked. "You just have to get used to the smell" he said, "The doors are open; you can pretend you are riding away from the smell."

I couldn't get used to the smell.

You see, as I have said, this house is something like 400 to 600 years old, and the stable has always been there. It looks now pretty much as it always has done, with the feeding troughs built into the wall and harnesses and saddles and all sorts of horsy type things hanging from everywhere. The only difference now is that the place is cleaner; the walls and ceiling have been painted and the floor has been tiled. And that is where the stink comes from, the floor. Because as a stable there was no floor; only earth that had been trodden hard by four hundred years of horse's hooves and soaked with four hundred years of horse's piss. And that piss smell cannot be contained by any form of flooring.
I managed fifteen minutes.

So then Stuart said something I thought no one would ever say.
He said, "I'll sort Ruth's bike out for you so you can go out on that."
Ruth's bike?
Ruth has a bike?
Ruth?
I don't think I said that out loud, but the shock must have shown on my face because Stuart laughed.
"Yeah, she's got one, never ridden it mind. I bought it for her when I bought mine, I had this idea that we could go out for days and have picnics by the river and do stuff together. But she won't go."
I felt sorry for him then. He had gone to the trouble of buying her a bike with the idea that they should share his passion for the things and spend quality time together, and she wouldn't even consider getting on it. She could have at least tried!
"I'm not sure," I told him. "It'll still be as hot and I like walking. I'll think about it. But thanks for the offer." Part of me thought he might like the bike being used, and part of me thought that he had bought it for her, so she should bloody use it. And I possibly shouldn't.

But still, that afternoon as I sat on my bed in the cool of my room I looked at the map on my phone to see where I could go. And that was when something happened.
It has happened a few times to be honest, maybe once or twice a year, and I don't usually mention it to anyone because most people think I'm mad. I believe that everyone has premonitions at some point, but they ignore them. I don't, I listen to them and I am often proved right if only to myself. I once sat in my car and argued with myself for refusing to travel the route I was about to travel. There was absolutely no need for me to go the long way around, I told myself. But I insisted and eventually I lost the argument and I won. And I went the long way around and avoided a pile up on the motorway that, had I gone that way, I could well have been in the very middle of. So, yes, I listen to my inner feelings.
I made the map bigger and smaller as I looked at villages and roads and where tracks came from and where they went. Then I decided to take pot luck. I made the map smaller again with our village in the centre of the screen and I lay the phone on the bed. I picked up a pencil and held it between my first finger and my thumb and held it over the phone, and I closed my eyes. I wriggled my hand a bit and then let the pencil slowly slide between my finger and thumb until the tip touched the phone.

It took a nanosecond, but it felt like a week. It wasn't like an electric shock, but it was a feeling. It came from the phone, through the pencil and up my arm. It forced its way over my shoulder and engulfed my torso. Within a second of the pencil tip touching the screen my heart started to race and I was almost struggling to breath. I started to sweat. I knew it wasn't a panic attack because the feeling was just bad. That's the only way I can describe it, it was bad. It was horrible and bad, really, really bad. I opened my eyes and stared at the phone. The pencil tip was touching a small village at the bottom of the screen. The map was too small for me to read the name so I made it bigger, and although I previously had no intention of letting on where I was in this story, I will mention the name I read. Alcudia de Crespins.

It was some distance from our village and I'm not too sure I would have made it there and back anyway; it was a bit over the distance range I had given myself. But there was no way I was going to try. The feeling was so bad that I needed to calm myself down so went to the window to open the shutters. The blast of hot air that forced its way into the room from outside didn't exactly help and I soon shut them again.

I did manage to calm down and even picked up the phone and looked at the map again, but I couldn't look at that village. As I write now, I still have no idea why I reacted so badly that day, but there was defiantly a reason why I should not go to Alcudia de Crespins and that feeling of 'bad' was so strong I even went and told Stuart that I had decided to continue walking and not take the bike. Maybe one day I will find out what caused that feeling, but I have Googled it and so far found nothing.

CHAPTER TEN

I got a message from a good friend in America saying that she had read how the Spanish/Portuguese border was to open on 6th of June. Sadly, as I was reading the article myself she sent another message. This one saying sorry, but she had now found the article to be false. Further investigation proved this to be the fact. Oh well, for a minute there I had been happy, and Karen was trying to help.
Then Ruth told me that the border was opening.
"I'm not too sure," I said, "A friend has just sent me that info, but when we both checked it proved to be false."
"I can fucking read, you know, and it said in the news that it is defiantly opening."
I shrugged and said, "OK, could you find that article and send me a link, please."
It took her two hours. To be fair I don't think she spent all of that time searching for it, just most of it. When I got the link and clicked on it I realized it was just someone's personal blog. Just some American woman who thought she knew what she was talking about. She claimed that the Portuguese beaches – not borders - were reopening and tourists would be allowed to visit them. But when I checked on a Portuguese news website it stated that only people who live within one kilometer of the few, named, beaches would be allowed to use them, and then only for exercise during certain hours. It seems that this one stupid woman had made her wild thoughts public and people who read it had believed her. Not only that, but they had then published their own daft thoughts, and we all know about the game of Chinese Whispers. My guess is that within an hour of the first idiot's blog, half of America possibly thought the pandemic was over.

I checked with the border force site and learned that they did not know when, or even if, the border would reopen. But apparently it was open in two places, twice a week, for an hour or so, to let essential workers through. I hoped those essential workers had a place to stay on both sides of the border and wondered about what strange hours they must work.

I had been sitting in the patio while reading and researching this information and Ruth came out to sit next to me with her coffee. To give her her due, when I explained that it hadn't been a news item she had found, but only someone's personal blog, she accepted that and she accepted what I told her I had learned via the Borer Force site.
"I've sent them an email anyway, to ask if it would be possible to cross if I paid for a covid test and it shows negative." I told her. (Yes, I was that desperate).
"Well, It's worth a try," she replied with a smile that made me nervous. She was being nice again and this usually meant there would be an explosion of idiocy later in the day.
And, sure enough, it came as I was preparing my dinner.

I had got a couple of margarine tubs filled with salad stuff out of the fridge when Ruth told me I couldn't eat it.
"Why not?" I asked.
"Well, not the onion anyway, it's poisonous."
I could feel my shoulders sag as I thought about the ridiculous claim that had been doing the rounds on social media for years about chopped onions being poisonous, and sure enough, that is what she told me.
I shook my head, "Sorry, but that's rubbish. I've been keeping chopped onions in the fridge and eating them for years. You can buy chopped onions in the supermarkets. It's just some idiot on Facebook doing a bit of scaremongering. Maybe an onion farmer trying to sell more onions, but more likely a school kid with nothing better to do."

Well, don't eat them then, at least," and she pointed to my strawberries.

"Why not?"

"They have worms in them."

"What?"

"All strawberries have worms in them, it's a fact. If you put them in water you'll see the worms coming out."

I put a strawberry in my mouth and ate it. "People have been eating them for thousands of years with no problems. Where did you hear about these worms?"

"It's a fact," she replied, "Try it for yourself."

So I did. I saved two strawberries and put them in separate cups. One I filled with warm water and one I filled with cold water. I left them while I ate my dinner and washed up, then I had a look.

No worms.

I took both cups to my room and left them overnight and checked again.

No worms.

Then I checked my Facebook and the very first thing I saw was a video of someone putting a strawberry in warm water and filming loads of little white worms coming out. I have to admit that it was a pretty convincing video and I wondered how they did it. But my strawberries still had no worms. Unfortunately I had wasted two of them, they did seem a big soggy when I fished them out of the water. I have no idea if those claims are true, or when they came from, but I am not going to give up eating strawberries because of flippin' Facebook.

******

Then something really nice happened.

I had been going to the village shop once or twice a week, they don't sell much, but fresh fruit is always welcome. And they did sell things like toilet roll and washing up liquid, which seemed to be the only things I was allowed to buy for the house. So I would go there to buy them before anyone else had a chance. On my little excursions to the shop or the recycling bin I had met a few of the locals. Most people must have worked out where I was staying and nearly all of them would smile and maybe say Hola, or even hello. When in the shop I would always attempt to use my very limited Spanish and I had been pleased to find that the shopkeeper was content to take the time to try and understand me. The more he allowed me to speak the more my confidence grew and the more I spoke. But still, I think it was mainly just me making odd sounds that he was able to make sense of.

Then one day I was waiting to be served, standing about a meter away from the lady in front. She was talking to a man beside her and they both turned to look at me. The man said something I did not understand so I smiled and shrugged and said "Lo siento, no entiento."

The man spoke again and this time I understood that he was saying something about the man behind the counter being funny. At least that's what I think he said. I think he must have been speaking Valencian to begin with and then switched to Spanish. But I still hadn't understood so I just shook my head and tried to look pleasantly apologetic.

But I did understand the man behind the counter as he told the couple that I was Italian.

"Italiano?" the man asked me.

"No, Inglesa" I said, and I was rewarded with two apologetic smiles and shrugs as the couple showed they did not understand English, and one rather surprised look from the shopkeeper who later told me he had been sure I was Italian.

People often think that Spanish and Italian are almost the same, but they are not. There are a lot of similarities and, I found I could speak to people in Italy because of my small amount of Spanish, but a lot of it is vastly different. (Mainly the speed; I could understand the Italians easier because they speak a lot slower.) So to have a Spaniard think I was Italian was quite a compliment. It meant I did not have that awful English accent that I hated so much but heard so often.
So I was happy as I went back to the house, and it was for that reason that I did not want to spoil things when I saw what Stuart was doing.

Stuart was boxing in the water pipe that ran from the tank, attached to the solar panel, to the bathrooms. It ran along the outside of the wall under the roof overhang and he spent a couple of days scaring the life out of me by climbing up the biggest ladder I had ever seen in a private household. As I wondered how on earth a private household manages to acquire one of these monsters, I watched him nail a length of thin wood to the underside of the roof so that it hung down enough to cover the pipe. Then he nailed another thin plank to the bottom of this to form a box around the pipe. Once each length was done he filled the space between the box and the pipe with expanding foam and I hoped there was never a leak in the pipe. This might sound like the ideal way to do it, but I noticed a problem. Stuart was using tongue and grove planks. Thin ones, the same type I had once used to line the ceiling in one of my vans. As I watched I saw that he was simply nailing through the tongue part of the plank, with the nails at an angle going into either the roof or the plank angled above the one he was attaching.
I am not a builder, and I am not a carpenter. Maybe this is the correct way to do it, but I couldn't help but wonder just how strong this whole thing was, and why he was using tongue and grove indoor planks.

Stuart nailed in his second plank of the day and then came down the ladder for a rest. He fetched his tea and sat at the table next to me.

"Is there a reason why you are using tongue and grove planks for this?" I asked.

"It's easier to nail on." He said.

I thought for a minute and then said. "I didn't realize you could use that wood outside. Has it been treated then?"

He stared at me in silence. Then he muttered something I couldn't make out and got up and walked into the stable. Later I saw all the remaining planks were piled up back in the stable and the work had stopped. No more boxing in was done while I was there. I never mentioned it again telling myself that the wood had been treated and Stuart had just got fed up of doing that particular job. I felt bad for him, I liked Stuart.

Later that afternoon I decided to soak my poor feet. I had a shower when I got back from my walks (against regulations, but Ruth gave in due to the fact that she didn't like the way I smelled) but my feet needed more attention.

Ruth gave me an old bowl she uses for 'grubby things' and I filled it with sun heated water from the hose pipe. Once it had cooled enough I poured in the bubbles and eased my feet in. Bliss.

Then along came Ginger. He was fascinated as I splashed about with my feet. First he watched, and then he tried to catch my feet. Then he chased some bubbles and then tried to 'catch' my feet again as if he were fishing. Stuart and Ruth also watched him for a while and when he got fed up and wandered off I went back to my book.

Later I washed the bowl and left it to dry in the sun, but when I went back to put it away it had gone. I looked around, scared in case I did something Ruth didn't want me to do, like lose the bowl or leave it in the wrong place. Then I saw it. It was on the floor, filled with water and with cat toys floating in it. When I asked Ruth about it she told me that it had looked like Ginger liked playing in water so she had left if filled with toys for him.

I said nothing. I couldn't think of anything to say. Ginger is a cat. Cats are known for not liking water. He had spent maybe three minutes wondering if my feet were fish worth catching and eating, and this woman seriously thought this meant he must like playing in water! Remember, this is someone who has had anything up to twenty cats at any one time over the past 35 years. Maybe every five million births a cat who loves playing with toys in bowls of water is born, but somehow I doubt it.

****

I had just finished my morning coffee and was about to scoop Linda from my lap and head out for my walk when Ruth appeared. "We are going shopping in a minute." She said. Knowing what her 'minutes' are like I wondered if I had time to do 8 or 10 kilometers before we went. But I didn't dare go. Had I not been back they would have gone without me or, worse, waited and given me the third degree when I got back. So I sat where I was and drank coffee for another hour and a half until we actually left.

The road workers were back at work as the Lockdown began to ease a bit more. And we saw that coffee shops and cafés were getting ready to reopen by placing their chairs and tables all along the path and even into the road as they attempted to keep people socially distanced. Because of this we found the roads a bit thinner in places. Turning a corner Stuart muttered, "That's a bit tight"

"No it fucking isn't," announced Ruth, "It's your fucking driving." Even sitting in the back seat I could see how tight it was, I'm still impressed that he managed to get around it without hitting anything. Then, for the entire journey she criticized him. This was actually quite normal, but this day it did seem a lot worse. She told him to speed up, to not go so fast, mind that cat, remember where to turn off, look out for that kid, change gear. She warned him what colour the lights were and said that there was no reason for him to get in a strop. I had once called her Hyacinth during a car journey but, although Stuart had snorted as he tried not to laugh, Ruth had not understood my meaning and so ignored me. (For those who do not know, look up an English TV show called Keeping up Appearances). This time I didn't need to defend him, he got his own back quite well.
"Those lights are red, you need to stop." She said.
So he stopped. There was no one behind us but two people on the pavement gave us a funny look. Stuart looked straight ahead.
Then another car pulled up behind us. After a minute the car gave a quick, light toot of its horn.
"Why the fuck is he honking?" Ruth demanded.
"Because we've stopped." Stuart said.
"But why is he honking?"
"Because the lights for this lane are green."
"So why the fuck are we sitting here?"
"Because you said we needed to stop."
Ruth looked around her and pointed to the traffic light that was red. "It's red." She announced.
"Yes, but that's for cars turning right, we are going straight on and our light is green. But you said we needed to stop and you know everything so I stopped."
By now our light had changed and I was grateful that the driver behind us wasn't arrogant enough to honk again. Maybe he thought we had a problem. We did, it was called Ruth.

"Well, fucking go then!" she screamed.
"Can't now."
"Why not?"
"Cos the lights have turned red now."
By this point I was also grateful I was sitting behind Ruth so she couldn't see as I slid, almost choking with laughter, down in my seat. The bravery of this man! I could hardly believe it. She was going to be unbearable for days after this, but it was so worth it.
And he did it again when we got home.

I had put everything away and then moaned at myself because I had forgotten to buy lemons.
"There's a fruit stall on the market. It's on today; you'll catch it if you go now." Stuart told me.
Before I had the chance to say anything Ruth put in her two-pennaeth worth.
"The market isn't open."
"Yes it is." He said.
"No. It is not!!"
"Yes. It is, I know it is."
"You don't know the market is on."
"Yes I do."
"No you don't."
"Yes I do, I got the WhatsApp."
"That was just to say it can open, you don't know if it is open."
"Yes I do."
"No you don't."
"Do,"
"Don't."
"Do, I saw it last week."
"Phtt! You saw nothing."
"I did, and I saw it this morning as we drove past the road."
"No you fucking didn't,"
"Yes, I fucking did."

It was at this point that I managed to leave unnoticed. I walked to the market, all three stalls of it, and I bought my lemons, happy to find that they were un-waxed so I wouldn't need to peel them.

On the way back I stopped off at the shop and treated myself to an ice-cream. I sat in the park to eat it, an excuse to stay out of the house longer. I felt I needed to stay away, just in case one of my hosts murdered the other and made me an accessory. I wondered where we could hide the body, and whose body it would be. Stuart had once told me that there was an old, dried up well under the floor of the back part of the stable. He had filled it in with rubble when the roof fell off part of the house and destroyed a wall - creating one of the roof terraces. He had jokingly told me that he had left a space big enough 'for her.'

As I sat in the park, under a tree, and trying desperately to eat my ice-cream before it became a drink, I thought about that house. There were so many places to hide a body. And with Ruth hardly ever leaving the house, if she disappeared it could be months before anyone noticed. If it hadn't been for her dad calling her from his home in Benidorm once a week Stuart could have done her in years ago. Maybe he was waiting for the old man to pop his clogs, but maybe he wasn't. Once again I was hit by the idea that Stuart must really, absolutely adore this horrible woman. Or he would have found an excuse and buried her along with that rubble under the stable floor.

I wondered if he had her insured.

******

I always knew when I was in for a grilling and a telling off because Ruth got out of bed before 11am. She must have spent the entire night awake and planning what she was going to say to me. In such cases she would get up just as I sat down in the breakfast/dining room with my coffee. Her timing was impeccable; I would be on my third or fourth sip as she would stomp past me on her way to the kitchen causing the cats to scatter. She would not speak, would not answer my "Good morning", would not make a noise other than the slap slap of what remained of her cheap flip flops against the hard skin of her feet. She would empty the hot water from the kettle, never trusting me not to use water from the day before that would have 'gone off' and refill it from the tap. I would hear it thumped back into its cradle and the lid slammed shut. Then there would be nothing else as it boiled. Sometimes I would hear the fridge door open, but often the sound of the kettle struggling to boil water through the scale would drown that out. She would then pour boiling water onto her instant coffee - even though I had once shown her the back of the jar where it states not to do this – and throw the spoon into the sink before stomping her way back to sit beside me.

One morning she decided to continue a conversation we had had more than ten years previously in Cornwall.

"When were you divorced?" she asked.
"2017."
"Why did it take so long?"
"Because I couldn't be bothered."
"So you didn't want to be divorced." It was a statement rather than a question.
"I really didn't care one way or the other. He's out of my life and that is all that matters."
"So who divorced who in the end?"
"He divorced me."
"Why didn't you do it?"

I knew what she was getting at and I was trying to stall. We had had this conversation before and I didn't want to have it again. But she was adamant.
"I told you," I said, "I really couldn't be bothered."
"You said once that you didn't want to pay for it."
Here we go, I thought.
I said. "That's right, it was going to cost £400 for the court fees alone, and he's not worth the money."
"But you know you don't have to pay for it." She said.
Another statement.
"I didn't, he paid for everything, I even asked for a stamp for the envelope because he's not worth the price of the postage."
"But he didn't need to pay for it either."
I took a deep breath, and then said, "We had this conversation ten years ago Ruth. Someone has to pay for it."
"No they don't, it's automatic." She had done it. She must have been waiting all night to say it and she had finally got it out. The fact that she believes that a divorce is automatic after a couple have been separated for more than two years. She had told me before that I didn't need to do anything or tell anyone. If I had been living apart from my husband for more than two years I was automatically divorced. Apparently this was 'The Law'. I have no idea where anyone could have got such an idea from and I had never had any intention of asking her. But she had been adamant ten years previously and I had believed that someone must have put her straight in the meantime. Possibly people had tried, but this is Ruth, and Ruth doesn't need to be told anything.
Now she ranted on and on about how I had wasted my time and money telling the court that I was divorced, because I was already divorced after two years. She kept saying "It's automatic," and whenever I said it wasn't she insisted that it was.
"When did you actually separate?" she demanded.
"2006"
"So, you have been divorced since 2008, not 2017"

"I think the court would disagree."
"The court is wrong."
Christ, this was unbelievable! I swear; I could not make this up.
I stared at my coffee. I really wanted to drink it but I also really wanted to throw it at her. How could anyone be this fucking stupid?
There was silence as I thought about it.
Stuart was divorced, so why didn't she understand the process?
Stuart was divorced.
Or was he?
Where had she got this stupid idea from?
Maybe……
Yes, it was possible. And the more I thought about it the more Stuart went up in my estimation. He may play the fool, but he's not a daft as he makes out. Well, not all the time anyway. I racked my brain for anything I might have heard about his ex wife, but I didn't remember anything about her being remarried or not. There was a chance that Stuart wasn't really divorced. Maybe he never bothered for the same reason I didn't. Maybe he had no intention of ever remarrying so it just didn't matter. Maybe he told Ruth this daft story to keep her quiet and stop her asking questions because he is not actually divorced.
It's a possibility.
I didn't bother with divorce because I didn't care, although I did plan on making a will so that if I had anything to leave my son would get it all. I never got around to it but what I did do was make sure my boy would have easy access to everything I owned and my husband would have no access at all. Then he started divorced proceedings so I let him get on with it. It took him nine years to file and then he got a lot wrong, like my age, and our last address. And my name.

It then took him two more years to get that right and hand over some piece of paper the court had asked him for. I was never sure what that was, but they told me they couldn't do anything without it.

Maybe Stuart was still married and that might mean that if he dies everything goes to his ex wife, or maybe his kids. Surly, if they bought this house together there would be provisions for Ruth if he died.

But maybe not.

The more I thought the more confused I got. I could see him not wanting to marry Ruth, but he clearly loved her. I could see him wanting to put his children first while they were little, but they were grown up now with kids of their own.

They must have talked of his divorce in the early days. It must have been he who had given her this ridiculous idea.

But why?

And, more to the point, why was she stupid enough to believe it?

But as I sat there thinking and trying to calm myself down she was building up for round two.

"Is your name real?"

"What?"

"Your name, it's a bit strange, is it real?"

"Ruth, I am a genealogist, I have traced my family tree back to the 1500's. Most of the Ebdells' were vicars during the 17th and 18th centuries, they went to college; and university; they could read and write. Yes, my name is real."

"But it's not your name, is it? It's not your family."

"Yes it is my name; I got it from my father."

"But then you got married, so you had your husband's name. Ebdell isn't your family name it's your husband's family."

"I told you ten years ago; - My husband's name is Smith, that was his family name. It shouldn't have been, but his great grandmother couldn't keep her knickers on. That was my married name. That is my son's name. I changed my name back to my maiden name, by deed poll, after we separated because I hated being a Smith and it was cheaper than divorce. I kept the Mrs because my boy asked me to. I was born an Ebdell and I'll die an Ebdell, it's my legal name."

But she didn't hear half of what I said because she was talking. Telling me that once I was married I couldn't just change my name 'willy nilly' and I was wrong for trying to use a name that didn't exist, and anyway, didn't I once say that my son's name was German? Why had I given my son a German name?

That was the only thing I responded to when I said, "My boy's middle name is German because my Mother-in-Law is German. That is down to choice."

"So……."

"So shut up Ruth," came a voice from behind me. It was quiet, but it was clear the speaker meant business.

"Oh fuck off!" she said. But it had worked. She left the room.

"You should just walk away from her," Stuart told me.

"Yeah, I know I should." And I did know, I also knew that it would do no good at all because she would probably follow me or just start on again the next time I saw her.

That day I walked late. I went to the river and walked along a track that I had found before but never investigated. It meant walking over a place where the rocks had fallen from above and looked like more were about to follow. But I was angry and needed something to make me work hard to calm me down. Climbing over those rocks in my crock flip flops and then my bare feet did the trick. I was exhausted, sweating and thirsty by the time I found a place to sit in the shade. I dangled my hot feet in the cool water, sipped the now warm lemon water from my bottle, and watched as the glass clear liquid flowed past on its never ending journey. After a while I found Israel Kamakawiwo'olw on my phone and let his gentle voice mix with the sound of the running water.
I closed my eyes.
Even when I can't understand the words Israel's voice always transports me straight to paradise.

CHAPTER ELEVEN

I had a very pleasant walk of about 10 kilometers one morning although I had no idea where I had been. I had just wandered off and got lost and when I realized it was possibly time to go back I got out my phone. This, I believe, is the main reason for a SatNav, so I can find myself when I deliberately get lost. I love to do this while driving as well as walking. That morning I had found several old and abandoned houses to look at as well as streams and little waterfalls and a very odd shaped tree growing at an angle. I also found an odd looking creature on the road and watched it for a while before taking a photo. Once back at the house I was able to Google the thing and learned that it was a Red Striped Oil Beetle.
I had my shower, made my lunch and sat down in the patio to eat.
And I heard a strange noise.
At first I thought it was the thump thump of someone dragging something heavy down the stairs and wondered which one of them was still alive. I had a mental image of covering a face with dirt and promising never to tell when Ruth yelled, "What the fuck are you doing?"
Dam, it wasn't her.

In fact both of them were still very much alive and healthy when I went into the main room to see what was going on. Ruth had appeared from the Breakfast/dining room and Stuart was clumping down the stone staircase wearing his usual pair of shorts. But instead of his usual sandals he had on a pair of brown leather cowboy boots that must have had studs in the heals, and a brown leather cowboy hat.

"Look what I found," he said, jumping from the bottom step and onto the stone floor with a clunk. Not exactly a James Cagney decent, I thought. He then proceeded to hook his thumbs into the belt loops of his shorts and hold his elbows out as he did a little tap dance around the room. Still very un-Cagney like. In fact, I have never seen Brokeback Mountain, but I thought Stuart might have fitted in quite well. I was almost roaring with laughter, the scene was hilariously funny, but Ruth was not amused. She stood, thin lipped, and watched until Stuart stopped moving, and then asked, "Where the hell did you find them?"

"In a cupboard I haven't looked in for years. I forgot I had them."

"Well, put them back and forget again." She told him, trying desperately to hide the grin that was sneaking its way across her face. They looked at each other for a moment and she actually smiled at him. And I saw the connection between them. I believe it's a connection that no one else will ever understand. Or ever want to. But whatever it is, it is very strong. And in all honestly I think that when one of them finally shuffles off this mortal coil, the other will follow shortly after. I just cannot see one of them living without the other and certainly no one else would ever have either of them!

****

We sat side by side in the breakfast/dining room and I was waiting for it to begin.
I didn't have to wait long.
"Where does your son live?" Ruth asked.
"Santiago"
"In Portugal"
"No, Santiago de Compostella, it's in Spain."
"Phht, are you sure."
"Yes, it's in Galicia"
"Stupid name, you made that up."
"Galicia is a province of Spain."
"I fucking know that. The other name, Santiago Compost, you made that up."
"No I didn't. It's a real city, it's a famous city it's where the walks go to."
"Who, what walks."
"The Camero. No, Camino, it runs along the top of Spain and ends in Santiago de Compostella."
"What the fuck are you on about?"
I gave up.
"My boy lives in Santiago de Compostella, that's in Galicia."
"That's in the north."
"Yes."
"So where does he live now?"
"Santiago de Compostella in Galicia"
"But you said it was near Portugal."
"It is, just north of it."
"North of What?"
"North of Portugal."
"How can it be north of Portugal? It's either in Portugal or it's in Spain."
I was getting a headache and needed another coffee. I said, "It's in Spain, in that bit that's just above Portugal."
"What do you mean above? How the fuck can it be above Portugal?" She was getting angry now.

"OK, think of a picture of Spain, think of it as a square shape." She was staring at me, but she nodded. "Uh huh!" she said.
"Now, you know where Portugal is?"
"Yes, but it's not in Spain."
"No, it's that bit at the side."
"Right." The eyes were glazing over; she had no idea what I was talking about.
"Well, the bit of Spain that goes over the top of Portugal, on the map, that's Galicia."
"Nothing goes over the top of Portugal. What the fuck are you on about? People running across Spain and things going over the top of Portugal? You're fucking mental. I only asked a simple question."
"OK, try this….you know when you look at the weather report on the telly?"
"Yes."
"When you see the map of Spain?"
"Yes."
"Well, it's a kind of square but with a piece missing from the left side."
Silence.
Blank face.
Staring eyes.
The lights were on, but there was defiantly no one home. I carried on… "That bit that's missing is Portugal, and the bit that's left, above the bit that's missing, is Galicia, or at least part of it."
The lights went out.
Then she shook her head and I think they came on again, or at least a candle was lit.
"You're talking out your fucking arse, you are." She said.
"You have no idea what Spain looks like and nothing is above Portugal."

I bit my tongue, I did not say it. I promise, I did not say that there was nothing above the neck on her body. I simply sat and stared into my empty coffee mug and she was quiet. I assumed she was staring at me. I could almost feel her eyes, could almost hear what she was thinking; 'she's mad, totally mad, she knows nothing, trying to tell me Spain is square!' I imagined her telling her sister, her only friend, "She's totally insane, she knows nothing, tried to tell me there's a place called Compost and that Spain has a part that goes over the top of Portugal."
How did she do it? I just couldn't understand how she managed to be so bloody stupid. And she honestly believed she knew everything. She had lived in that country on and off for twenty years, and didn't even know what shape it was. Most nights she had looked at the weather report on the TV, actually looked at that little map of Spain, and she had not understood what she was looking at.
How does anyone do that?
I've read about people like Ruth in horror stories. People who live in a world of their own; who never go outside their front door and who murder anyone who visits the house. I felt I was probably very lucky to be alive even though I often thought that death would be a pleasant release from this situation.

Then;
"When did you walk across the top of Spain?" it was said with the utmost sarcasm.
"I have never walked across the top of Spain." I said.
Knowing what was coming.
"Well, what were you on about then, when you said about walking across it."

I tried not to sigh, "There's a path. I don't know exactly where it starts, but I think it's by the French border somewhere, and it runs right along the top of Spain, I think close to the coast and it ends up in Santiago de Compostella at some church. I think it's a kind of religious thing to be able to walk it. It's called the Camino Trail."
"So how do you know about it?
"I watched a film."
"A film?"
"Yes, it's called The Way. I think it's Martin Sheen who does the walk, well, the bloke he plays does it."
"It must take days!"
"About a month I think, if you're fit enough."
There was silence for a bit as I waited for what was coming next. Then…
"I thought you once said that religious walk was in Portugal because your boy did it."
"Yes, there is one that starts in Lisbon I think, and it goes north to the same church." I decided not to mention the one that starts in Ireland; she would never cope with that.
"And did he do it all?" she asked.
"No, he broke his foot so he had to stop, and his mate had to go back to wherever it was he came from."
"But if the walk is from Lisbon, how come it ends in Spain? It doesn't make sense."
"Because you can walk over the border. Usually."
Oh gods I wished I could walk over that border right there and then. I would have walked to Santiago first if only I could have got out of that house.
That conversation ended quietly. It was clear from the smirk on Ruth's face that she hadn't believed a word I had said. She was totally convinced that I was utterly insane. I was happy to let her think it just as long as she left me in peace to finish my coffee.

Later that day Ruth decided to teach me how to cook eggs. Not wanting to spread my single fried egg out over the ten inches of the frying pan the previous day, I had tipped the pan so that the egg and oil all sat neatly on the bend of one side. Buy sitting that side on the flame I had always been able to fry an egg the way I like it. Slowly, with enough depth to taste it, and with no crispy bits around the edge.

But Ruth was horrified when she saw what I had done and now she was determined to 'teach me to do it properly'.

First she warmed the pan and then added oil. Then she went to get the eggs out of the fridge and I watched the pan as the oil got hotter and hotter. I swear, I thought she was going to make an omelet or teach the local fire crew how to deal with a house fire. And the oil got even hotter. Finally she cracked an egg into the pan and I stepped back to avoid the spitting oil. I watched as the edges of the egg turned black. Another egg hissed and spat as it too was thrown into the boiling oil. Then a splatter guard was put on top of the whole thing.

Yes, seriously, a splatter guard for eggs. I have never even used one for sausages; in fact I have never actually used a splatter guard for anything, ever. I have never needed to. And here she was, using one for eggs!

After a second or two the guard was removed and put into the sink. The pan was lifted from the hob and two strange looking things were scooped out and onto a plate.

It was clear they had once been eggs because the yellow bit was showing under a film of clear goo. The clear goo tried to reach the white of the egg, but there wasn't really much white left to reach, it was black and curled and bubbled and possibly has hard as the cooled volcanic rock it looked like. The plate was waved under my nose. "There," she said, "That's how to cook eggs properly." And then she stomped off to put the plate in front of Stuart who sat for a moment staring at it before looking up at her. Without words they looked at each other. Without words I know she told him to 'Fucking eat it'. Without words he did.

But if I had thought that was bad I was in for a surprise when she did cook an omelet. She knows the oil has to be hotter for an omelet. Do I really need to explain the stink that managed to find its way out of the kitchen, through the main room and the three inch thick wooden doors to the street beyond? I was just grateful I didn't have to wash the pan afterwards!

****

Stuart and I sat at the table in the back garden talking about history. Ruth wandered out, sat down and listened for a bit, realized she had no idea what we were talking about and left again. But then Stuart's phone beeped so she came running back to find out who had contacted him and why, and what they had said, and to tell him how to respond. It was the woman who owned the smaller house next door, and the poor cat who was still living there and crying as she watched the others from the rooftop.
The woman was letting them know that her house was now for sale and both cats would be 'removed' as soon as possible. Well, one of them had already been removed, and neutered, and had made himself very comfortable and would be going precisely nowhere. The other one I worried about. I hoped she would go to a nice home but somehow I doubted the owners would care enough to see to that. I had a suspicion that Stuart's ladder might get another airing before the house was sold, but I said nothing. Had I had my van I would have stolen her and taken her with me. But I didn't have my van, so there was nothing I could do.

But Ruth wasn't interested in what was going to happen to the cats, she was only interested in the house and how it was being advertised. She claimed she wanted to see what it was like inside, as if Stuart and I didn't know that she had already been all over the building and had a good look anyway. A few minutes later I found her sitting at a table inside with her laptop open searching houses for sale in the village. And she had found it. "Come and look at this," she instructed me. So I did.

Estate agents in Spain take a totally different attitude to selling to that of estate agents in England. I've bought and sold property in England and I know that an average estate agent can photograph Nelson Mandela House and by the time the photo is published it resembles Windsor Castle. We all know that in agent speak the word 'Spacious' means the average man can't quite reach the north and south walls at the same time, and a bedroom is classed as a double if it is more than six feet wide. We know that 'in need of decoration' means the back wall is possibly missing and 'Some attention needed' means the place is possibly condemned. I once went to view a house that boasted a conservatory only to find it was actually half a shed that was leaning against the back wall.
But in Spain they tell and show the truth, if they can be bothered. I have seen many properties for sale with just a photo of the outside, and by this I really do mean just the outside; sometimes there is no photo of the house at all. If there are photos of the inside they are often taken with a mobile phone as the agent hurries to count bedrooms. Occasionally they might be checked before uploading to the internet, where I think they possibly filter the better ones out. The advert for the house next door had several photos possibly taken on a Samsung Sharp and without any lights on. Several pictures of the 'garden' looked like they had been taken by accident as the agent slipped on the cat shit and they all showed the place in its full horrifying glory.

"Crikey" I said, "That's going to take a while to sell."
"A house always takes two years to sell in Spain," said Ruth, "They never go any quicker."
"I'm not surprised if that's how they advertise them." I said.
"It's got nothing to do with the advertising, "she snapped, "Houses just don't sell for at least two years."
And that was when I made my mistake for that day. When I said, "My brothers sold my dad's place in a couple of months." But I saw her stiffen so I added, "Maybe it's different in Tenerife."
"They must have sold it for less than half of what it was worth then."
"Nope, they got a good price, my brothers' aren't daft."
"Yes they are," she informed me, even though she hadn't known until that precise moment that I even had two brothers, "They must have let it go cheap or it wouldn't have sold before two years." She snapped the laptop shut and I took that as my cue to leave and escaped back into the garden. The truth is that I have no idea how long it took to sell my father's apartment but it certainly wasn't two years, and I have no idea how much they got for it because I never felt the need to ask. The place was sold to pay for my father's care and that was all any of us were really interested in.
****

Ruth told me about something she had seen on the internet about a man being killed by police in Manchester. Having just read about a similar incident in America I asked her if she was sure it was Manchester. Of course she was fucking sure; she's not a fucking idiot. She went to school, she learned how to fucking read! While she was explaining this to me she was flicking through her phone until she found what she was looking for. She turned her phone towards me to show me the article but I wasn't close enough to be able to read it. However, the photo was as clear as day. An American police car.

I guess a Chinese person, or maybe someone from Africa or Japan might mistake an American police car for an English one, but I found it hard to believe that an English person would. I reminded myself that this was Ruth I was talking to and leaned in to have a closer look. Then I made that day's big mistake. "It says Minnesota," I said.

"It says fucking Manchester!" she said, whipping back the phone to look at it herself. "Your problem is that your eyes are fucked. It's because you sit out here reading on your phone all the time. You shouldn't do all that reading, you should sit inside and do it. And not on your phone, you should read real books instead."

I decided to wander off; I really didn't want to be anywhere near her when she realized she had been wrong.

But she didn't realize, or at least she didn't admit it. For the rest of the day she talked about the man who was killed by police in Manchester and it wasn't until the world went mad a few days later that she stopped saying it.

In the meantime I scoured the internet for information on the Spanish/Portuguese border. I had read that Valencia might be going into phase three of coming out of lockdown in a few days time and that if we did, we might be able to travel. When I next spoke to someone at the embassy I asked if they knew anything. They didn't, but they didn't hold out much hope for me being able to move to a town close to the border either. I was told to try and stay put for now because it could be another month.

Some reports said that the border would be open in the middle of June, and others said the beginning of July. The airlines still had nothing flying and the trains and busses were still stationary. I'm not one for making plans because plans very rarely work out, but right then I just wanted to be doing something about leaving.

I wanted to be leaving. But there was nothing I could do.

I wandered back out into the garden and found Stuart sitting alone and we started chatting. Somehow we got into the subject of driving lorries, both of us having driven them around London. But Stuart told me a story of something that happened to him elsewhere. I'm not 100% sure I believe this story, but I am going to repeat it anyway, because it's funny.

There were three men in the lorry, a driver and two passengers. Stuart was one of the passengers. They were on their way to their last drop of the day when a stone pinged up from somewhere and hit the windscreen. The screen shattered but did not collapse. The driver managed to pull over to a safe place and stopped the vehicle.
The three of them sat and wondered what to do. The windscreen was a mass of cracks and no longer transparent so the lorry could not be driven. The only thing they could do would be for one of them to walk along the road and find a phone box to call the company. Then they would have to wait for someone to come out and collect the lorry and give them a lift back. They would have to add this last drop to the next day's delivery. But thinking again, no, they couldn't add it to another delivery. Because that day was a Friday and on the Monday they would be going in another direction. They realized they would be made to load the goods onto another lorry and head out and do the delivery no matter how late it made them finishing the day. And this was a Friday night they were about to miss out on. They all just wanted to do the last delivery and get off home.
So a decision was made.

The driver found a hammer from somewhere and smashed out the glass. While he was clearing shards from the rubber the two passengers swept up the rest of the glass and felt they had done a good job. Even though everyone who got into the lorry for the next year found a piece of glass somewhere, at the time the three men thought they had done well. The glass was swept into a bag and got rid of. Stuart didn't say where they got rid of it and I didn't ask. I prefer to think they found a bin. Next the driver rummaged around in a tool box and found a pair of safety goggles which he put on. The three of them did their coats up and off they set.

Stuart told me he couldn't see a thing, he couldn't even open his eyes. He said, "When you see in the movies how the hero smashes out the glass and carries on driving, it's crap. That's not possible. The only way we were moving was because the driver had goggles on."

Things were flying everywhere; everything that wasn't actually screwed down was immediately thrust out into the atmosphere, never to be seen again. Wind was coming in the front, whipping around the cab and pinning them to their seats before being forced out again. The noise was deafening. After a few minutes someone decided it might be better if the side windows were open, and this did make things a little easier as now the wind had somewhere to go, And Stuart was able to open his eyes a little. He did so just in time to see what his mate was doing.

Stuart was sitting close to the door and his mate was in the middle, closer to the driver and the man's foot was moving. Stuart watched as the foot reached over to the button on the floor in front of the driver's seat. The foot pushed.

And the air turned blue as cold soapy water was forced into the cab and all over the drivers face and body. He swore and cussed and tried to wipe the goggles with the sleeve of his leather jacket while the other two were struggling to hold onto the passenger seat as they rolled about with laughter. And then Stuart noticed the wiper blades; bent inwards with the force of the wind they looked like a giant spider trying to get into the cab. He found it very difficult to laugh with all that wind in his face, but he couldn't help it.

Soon they arrived close to the destination and the lorry slowed as they drove through the built up area. With the wind in the cab no longer so fierce they were able to relax a bit and to the average passerby it looked like nothing was wrong. Until Stuart and his mate started leaning out through the windscreen hole to wave at people while the driver giggled behind his goggles. They arrived at their destination looking none the worse apart from the new hairstyles they were all sporting. They delivered the goods and set of back to the yard. They were doing about 60 miles an hour when Stuart saw that his door was not closed properly so he opened it to give it a good slam. Under normal circumstances when the wind is only on the outside of the vehicle the door will slam itself shut almost immediately. But this time the wind was inside the vehicle and the door was flung outwards away from the cab. And there it stayed, flapping about with Stuart hanging off it like something from a Charlie Chaplin movie. Stuart could not really describe what happened next because he couldn't remember. The only thing in his head at the time was the fact that he was going to die. He was slightly conscious of the fact that his feet were possibly still in the cab and someone was grabbing onto them, but he couldn't be sure. After what felt to him like ten years, but was probably only a few seconds he was dragged back into the cab, he thinks by his belt, brining the door with him. Even then, it took the two of them to get it to shut properly.

The only real problem they had was that it was their turn to pick up the Friday Fish and Chips to take back to the yard for all the other drivers. They did this, but as they handed them out the others complained that their dinner was cold.

****

Then the world went mad.
People were stamping their feet and throwing temper tantrums all over the pace. I saw a video of a riot in London and heard one plonker shout "That's for the one you killed" as he threw something at a policeman. A policeman in London; who had possibly never been to America and probably couldn't find Minnesota on a map if it was pointed out to him. Maybe it's because I don't read the news but I just didn't get the connection. I didn't understand why people in England, Spain and the rest of Europe needed to make such a fuss about something that happened on the other side of the world, to someone they didn't know existed until they saw a biased edited Facebook clip about him.
I did a little research and saw several different videos of the same incident and I made my own mind up that both parties were at fault. Yes, it was bad that someone had died and yes, I did feel a murder had been committed and the murderer should pay, but if one man hadn't been such a twat in the first place the incident wouldn't even have happened.
This is just my opinion and I am just a little person who has never been to Minnesota and doesn't really care what happens there.
Selfish?
Possibly, but a lot less stressful.
It was even less stressful for Ruth because she didn't believe it had ever happened.

Oh, she believed a man had been killed by a policeman, and she even now admitted that it didn't happen in Manchester. But the riots were, according to Ruth, all in my imagination. No, they never happened. She had not seen it on the news so I must be wrong. I stared at the back door of the house while she gave me her opinion of the BBC news and police tactics and racial hatred, and boy did she have an opinion! I cannot repeat it here because I don't know what she said because I wasn't listening. I just let her talk as I watched a feral tom cat walk over the roof tops and drop down into the yard of the house next door and two other cats pad about the roof top, walking in circles as if waiting their turn. As Ruth talked about there being no Africans in the war I began to fantasize about cats running brothels and how many mice the little thing next door might be charging.

Hang on a minute.

"What? Ruth, did you just say there were no Africans in the war?"

"Well, there weren't. They were all in Africa."

"Which war are you talking about?"

"The fucking world war!"

"So, You're saying that all Africans were in Africa during the two world wars?"

"Yes!" she said it as if she were fed up of trying to explain the truth to an idiot. And maybe she believed she was because all I could think of to say was "OK."

I went back to watching the cats as she continued talking. My mind hurt when I tried to understand the creature sitting beside me. In my mind I scratched off the words Opinionated Covert Narcissist and wrote the words Utter Fucking Retard.

This was confirmed the next day.

I was just taking my third sip of my morning coffee when the slap slap of her flip flops echoed through the Breakfast/Dining room. Linda jumped off the table and headed for the door as they slapped their way into the kitchen and I heard the sound of the kettle being emptied and refilled to the top. I heard the clunk as it was slammed onto its base and the click as it was turned on. Then came the noise of the draw being opened and a spoon being taken out followed by the draw sliding closed and the clatter of spoon and coffee jar. The fridge door was opened and closed twice as milk was fetched and returned and then the draw opened again. Why, I wondered, was she opening the cutlery draw for the second time? I heard rustling and then the draw closed again and I understood. The rustling was chocolate wrapping. Crikey, even I can't eat chocolate before my morning coffee.
It was only just coming up to nine o'clock and she was already up so I knew I was in for the third degree. She had been awake all night thinking about something she either needed to tell me or something she would demand to know. I was already late for my walk and now I knew I was going to be heading for the river fairly soon to try and pretend the world did not exist.

Her bum was not even on the chair when she started.
"Why did you take that job selling motorhomes if you didn't like it?"
"I needed a job."
"But you said you hated it."
"Yes."
"So why didn't you leave?"
"I needed the money, I had a child to feed and clothe."
"Huh. My sister had four kids and raised them alone and never did a job she didn't like."
"She was lucky."

"No. She was right. You don't have to do a job you don't like. That's what benefits are for. They are not going to let you go hungry if you've got kids to feed."
"That's not what benefits are for." And I got up planning on leaving.
"Yes, they are, you don't know what you're talking about."
I fell for it, just as she knew I would. But I didn't get angry enough to shout. I spoke calmly, but with force.
With one hand on the table so I leaned over her I said, "Firstly, benefits are not there just for people who can't find a job they actually like and, secondly, yes they bloody do let you go hungry and you bloody do know that they did it to me and my boy. So why can't you let it drop?"
"My sister said….."
"I don't care what your sister said. You know full well what happened to me, I told you ten years ago. But I am not ill now and I am not on benefits. It's history, so drop it." I stood upright and headed out of the door.

I have no idea why Ruth feels the need to do things like this. Why she thinks she can drag up the past all the time and tell me that she thinks I did something wrong twelve or fifteen years ago, when she didn't even know me.
I went out into the blazing heat and walked to the river. Then I walked alongside the river until I came to a shallow part where I walked across it. I climbed up the bank on the other side and stumbled my way through bushes and trees until I came out at a quiet spot I had found a couple of weeks ago. By the time I sat down on a huge stone in the shade I was sweating and tired. Alone I sat and I tried to let my mind go blank. I did not want to think about the situation I was in at that point, let alone the one I had been in fifteen years ago. The past is the past, and I like to let it stay there. My present was bad enough.

Yes, I thought, I know I am safe and things could have been so much worse. I could have been stuck in the van in England in the cold. I could have been stuck in the van in Portugal, inside Raymond's garage, in a village where no one speaks English. But here I was, living free except for food; safe and warm. And able to get out and sit by the river and pretend the world did not exist. But Ruth was driving me insane. I really felt I was beginning to understand why some people kill. Although I hadn't got to that point and I hoped I never would. I know we all say things like 'I wouldn't pee on him if he were on fire' but we don't usually mean it. There is one man who I would happily stand by and watch take a beating. I wouldn't do it myself, but I wouldn't call an ambulance or the police either. I could watch, and then walk away. But this is a man who deliberately set out to hurt my child. I knew I couldn't watch Ruth take a beating, but if I went back to the house and found her dead I would certainly step over the body to make a coffee.

CHAPTER TWELVE

On Friday June 12th we learned that travel between most of the provinces would reopen on Monday 15th, not all provinces, just some of them. Brussels also announced that all borders, including Spain/Portugal, would reopen the same day. But Spain announced they would open their borders on the 22nd and Portugal said July 1st. I wondered if Portugal just wanted to get rid of a few people while not letting anyone else in. I didn't blame them but I was really disappointed, I had hoped to be able to leave on the Monday but it wasn't going to be possible. There were still no hotels open that I could afford and still no planes or trains. Without some sort of guarantee that the border was going to open I didn't dare risk leaving for a hotel. I could afford a week, but no longer. And I needed some of the cheaper places to reopen. Stuart must have realized I wasn't happy. "I'll have a look on the Dark Web," he said, "Find someone who will smuggle you over the border."
"OK," I said, "But I don't have much money so you'll have to offer your body as payment."

Reading the other news didn't exactly make me feel any better. Statues were being torn down, police were being abused, and people were even being killed. Some wanted to change history by pretending the slave trade didn't happen (personally I believe that if your ancestors were slaves then you should be immensely proud of them, of their sheer determination to survive under the worse of conditions. I am sure they didn't fight for their freedom just for people to now pretend they didn't) and everyone was afraid of being called a racist.

From America I read about insults to a solider called Sgt. William Harvey Carney who had won some sort of medal. I Googled him and learned that he was a hero of the 54th Massachusetts Regiment from the civil war. A monument to the regiment had been defaced by people shouting something about Black Lives and how they hated white people. But my reading had shown me that the 54th was a regiment of black soldiers, so I just didn't understand what was going on. I have never understood racism anyway, but now I was really confused.

I saw that some people were claiming that a statue of Churchill must be removed because he had been raised to believe he was better than black people. The fact that he had also been raised to believe he was better than most white people was totally ignored. But I read it didn't matter anyway because Boris had already had him boarded up.

I read that books, movies and TV programmes from the past were being banned and white people were apologizing for having done comedy shows where they dressed up as black people. I asked when Eddie Murphy would apologize for dressing up as a white person, but I was ignored.

One woman complained about someone selling cotton because it was 'reminisant of the slave traid' so I asked for Rome, Athens, most of Egypt and the pyramids to be dismantled because they too were mostly built by slaves.

A friend of mine in England popped onto the page and told me that I shouldn't wear my hair in braids any more just in case she decided to feel offended, and I told her I would stop just as soon as she stopped eating fish and chips. She told me she probably shouldn't make me any more mango puddings, and I told her I probably shouldn't bring her any more pear cider. She said she wanted me to give back the coconut shell spoons her brother had made for me and then, because a stranger popped into the conversation and tried to make it serious, she added "And while you're at it you better give my brother back too."

I replied, "Naff off, I'm defiantly keeping him," which got a heart reaction from the man himself.

****

That Sunday I was up early and out of the house before Ruth could get up and pounce on me with any kind of question. I went to the river and spent a happy couple of hours with Jack Reacher. I am not a fan of Tom Cruise and have never seen the films. But I am a big fan of Lee Childs and the Jack Reacher of the books. To my mind he is the perfect husband. Tall, broad, strong, protective and never home. Even when he is around he doesn't expect a woman to cook and never has any laundry. The perfect man.
So I enjoyed my morning.

When I got back to the house Stuart told me that it had been announced that the border defiantly won't be open until July 1st. But that was only the land border, the air and sea borders were open. I could go by boat or fly in, but I couldn't drive or walk. Stuart had found me a flight for £9.99 to Porto on the 24th. I could then take the train to the village, he said. Ruth had found that the train from Porto to Portalegre takes just five hours so they said I could be back in the village in no time, and it was really cheap.
I checked it out.
The flight left from Madrid and, according to the websites, there were no trains for busses yet. Never mind, I thought, it's just a short walk of some 450 kilometers.
The flight lands in Porto at 3.30 in the afternoon and the one and only train leaves at 6 the following morning. So, pay for transport from the airport to a hotel then roughly £50ish for the night and pay for transport to the station in the morning.
Arrive in Portalegre a half an hour after the bus leaves for the village. So another night in a hotel and another 6 am bus to the village.
I tried to explain all this to them both but neither of them would understand. Ruth insisted on finding the train online and she showed me where it states that it takes five hours. "See," she said, "It can be done in one day."

"Yes," I said, "But there is only one train a day and it leaves before the flight lands so I would have to stay in a hotel for the night."
"No you don't, it can be done in one day."
"How?"
"Because the train only takes five hours."
I gave up.
I sat next to her and tried to book the train trip. I wasn't actually going to pay; I just wanted it to show everything to prove my point. That was when I found that it those five hours were also split over two days, so that meant three nights in hotels. And when I tried to actually book it nothing worked.
I tried to book a bus, but it wouldn't work. I tried to book busses and trains in Spain but it wouldn't work. "There's something wrong with your phone." Said Ruth when I mentioned it.
"They are not running yet." I said.
"Of course they are fucking running. It says so right there." She tapped her phone with her finger.
"They are not running yet." Said Stuart still looking at his own phone. He had been quiet for a while and I had wondered what he was looking at. Now he told us. He had learned that the time tables were all old, and that new ones would go live next week, on the 22nd. I wouldn't be able to book anything to anywhere until the websites were updated.
"That's a shame," he added, "You'll miss out on that cheap flight if you're not quick enough."
Oh gods. A train to Madrid and possibly a hotel there; then two trains, one bus and three hotels in Portugal, all because a flight is £9.99. Why couldn't they see the extra costs?
I went back to my room and looked at the way I wanted to go.

I wanted to fly to Badajoz and maybe stay there until the border opened. I could walk to the village from there, or I could get the bus. I could *see* the bloody village from there. And it would be cheaper to stay in a hotel there than it would be in Porto and a lot less stress than looking for three different hotels and two trains and a bus.

I even found a hotel. It looked nice and clean and was a decent price. It had a 24 hour reception so I considered it to be safe, and it was in the centre of the town and close to the river. There would be plenty of places to walk and places to eat. I also thought that to fly to Porto or Lisbon was likely to be busy. Hundreds of people had been waiting for the borders to reopen so the usual routs would be busy and hotel prices would be high.
And if I could walk, there was a slim chance I might get over the border early.

I wrote an email to a friend in Israel about my plans, and the following day I got a response saying that my plans to escape across the border sounded like something from a movie. "But then, your whole life sounds like a movie" he said "While I just stay here and dig up dead people." (He is an archeologist).

******

I had no idea where I was, I was just walking. The sun was hot and I was happily sweating. I hoped I was sweating off all the chocolate I'd been eating. I was passing what looked like allotments and spotted a man leaning on a spade smoking a cigarette. I smiled at him and he waved back. Then he left his spade standing in the earth and started to walk towards me with a cabbage in his hand. When he spoke it was slow and careful. I think he said something like, "I know you are English and don't understand but I want you to have this cabbage." And I must have got that right because as I took the cabbage and said "Gracias" his smile got even wider. I was really pleased, not just because someone had given me a cabbage, but because he had known I am English. Clearly he was from the same village and possibly knew who I was or at least where I was staying. It was a funny feeling; it was as if I had been accepted.
When I got back to the house Ruth was upstairs so I only spoke to Stuart who was sitting in the walled patio. "Fancy cabbage for lunch?" I said, plonking it on the table.

"I could make some coleslaw." He said, "Haven't had that for ages." So I put the vegetable in the rack in the stable where they keep things like that. And I immediately regretted it because of the smell of horse piss. I decided to say that I didn't like coleslaw after all.

"There's a cabbage in the stable, where did it come from?" Ruth managed to make that sound like she had found a dead horse in the bedroom instead of an innocent vegetable in the vegetable rack.
"Oh, I put it there; Stuart is going to make coleslaw."
"You didn't go shopping, where did you get it?"
I wondered if I should call a lawyer but she hadn't actually read me my rights yet so I told her.
"An old man gave it to me."
"Who? What old man?"
"I don't know, just a man who was working on his allotment as I walked past."
"What allotments? Where? There aren't any allotments here."
"I don't know, It was just a nice man who wanted to be friendly."
"Phtt! I don't think so."
I took a deep breath as quietly as I could and held it until she had gone back into the kitchen which, thankfully, wasn't long. I scooped Linda from the floor and put her on my lap where she sat expecting attention, and decided that I possibly should not mention the lady who had given me the two oranges the previous week. I had gone to the river to eat them knowing I would need a wash afterwards. They were always so lovely and sweet and juicy when they were straight off the tree. It's very rare I bother with oranges in England, there is no point. Not after having had them straight from a tree in someone's garden in Spain or Portugal. I don't know if they are a different species, but they certainly taste like it, and the lemons from Raymond's garden made the best lemonade I have ever tasted.

The following day when I got back from my walk and had disentangled Ginger and Linda from my legs, Stuart asked me if I could go back out because he had run out of carrots for the coleslaw.

****

On Saturday 20th we got the news I had been waiting for. We would be free of restraints on the following day. I read that the busses and trains wouldn't be running their normal schedule at first but that they would publish their time tables as soon as they could. The land border still wasn't going to open until the 1st of July but I found a hotel in Badajoz and looked for flights. There was nothing yet. As I was doing this Ruth appeared.
"Anything interesting?" she asked.
"Yes, defiantly. We are free as of tomorrow, we are out of lockd……"
"Monday."
"Oh, it says here, Sunday."
She leaned over me to look at my phone so I went to History and found the tab with the article on it and opened it to show her. "See, Sunday 21st at 12am." I read.
"Yes," she said, "Monday."
"Umm, That's an S and a U, it says Sund…."
"No, you're wrong. AM means after midnight so it means Monday morning. The 22nd."
" What?"
She stood up straight, took a deep and exasperated breath, placed her hands somewhere near where her hips possibly were, sighed and then said, "You really are stupid aren't you? AM means After Midnight and PM means Pre Midnight. So 12am on Sunday means Monday morning"
I just stared at her, possibly with my mouth open, totally gobsmacked.
She smiled. Well, it could have been a smile, I'm not sure; it looked a bit like a smirk, but whatever it was, she was sure she had taught me a lesson.

Once again I couldn't think of anything to say. The words 'are you sure your parents weren't father and daughter' didn't seem like a good idea and my brain couldn't take in the fact that she was actually serious so I just sat stationary with my mouth open while she walked away in triumph. Then I went to the shop and bought some chocolate.

When I got back they were both sitting in the patio with coffee, it seemed rude not to join them but I was a bit nervous as I sat down. However, Stuart was in a good mood and we chatted about nuclear power waste (you have to know this man). Then he mentioned the name of a town in Spain. I recognized it as one being close to where my son had once lived. But Ruth decided that he had pronounced the name wrong and tried to correct him.
"It's Sulu,"
"No, It's Salou."
"Sulu."
"Salou"
"Sulu!" she shouted.
Calmly Stuart told her that Sulu was in Star Trek and the name of the town was Salou."
"Oh fuck Off! I'm fucking sick of being fucking corrected all the time." I had not corrected her that morning, I had been too stunned to think of anything to say so maybe Stuart had heard the conversation and put her right.
He and I chatted while she tightened her lips and studied her phone. I hoped she was looking up the meaning of am and pm. Then the doorbell rang.

It was the woman who lived next door. Even though we were not meant to leave the province until the following day (or the day after, according to Ruth) she had driven over from her other home in Barcelona anyway and popped in for a visit now that she was back. Ruth ushered her through the house and into the patio. As the woman sat down Ruth asked "Do. You. Want. Agua?" and seemed pleased when the neighbour shook her head. Ruth thought she meant no thanks, but by the look on the poor woman's face I believe she was wondering what on earth had been said because I knew that she spoke no English. I also thought it might have been nicer if Ruth had offered her guest a coffee or maybe a cup of tea (or possibly gin in preparation for coping with Ruth). Maybe she could have got the china cup and saucers out as she had done for Daan and Jose. But maybe this poor neighbour wasn't rich enough for Ruth to want to impress. I think I was expected to move but I didn't, I had my coffee and I had a cat on my lap so I was going nowhere.

The three of them chatted and I was pleased to learn that I could understand most of what was being said. Stuart speaks good Spanish, even if he does have a really strong English accent, and he understands everything. But Ruth doesn't, although she claims to be almost fluent. She did occasionally say full sentences but her words were very basic, they were the sort of sentences I would say, and I don't think I speak Spanish at all! I listened to how this woman has the house for sale but isn't really sure she wants to sell it. Ruth told her it would be "Mucho, mucho, time to vende" and I knew exactly what was going through the woman's mind as I watched the stunned expression on her face. Ignoring Ruth she turned to Stuart and I listened to how she had continued to teach during the lockdown by using the internet and having the whole class online together. And then I listened to her explaining how that works because Ruth had assumed that meant "solo to solo" teaching. And I listened as she explained to Stuart that the kids would put a hand up if they wanted to speak, just as in a normal classroom, because he had thought they would all speak at once. Then Gail walked past and the woman recognized her. So the conversation about cats began.
This poor woman was made aware that both Ginger and Gail had originally been her cats, that Ruth had rescued them and they were now living here and that she had been feeding the other female every day. This took some time to explain due to the many hand movements and English words. I waited until I saw offence in the woman's face as Ruth used her very own form of spanglish to explain that she (Ruth) had had to look after the cat because she had to! Because the other woman didn't know how to, and that was when I got up and left.

Regardless of the fact that this woman didn't care about her cats, Ruth was in the process of telling her she didn't know what she was doing and I guessed the poor woman was about to learn how utterly useless she was compared to the sainted Ruth. I didn't not want to be involved so I took my washing off the line as an excuse to leave the table and went to my room until I heard the woman leave.

Later, in the breakfast/dining room Stuart was talking about quantum physics and I said that it was just going to go over my head as I know nothing about it. I was pretty sure that he didn't either, but that was not going to stop him talking about it. Ruth said she couldn't even spell it, which made me grin and I felt that the morning's temper must have abated. Stuart went on to tell us how we could exist in two different places at once and that it had been proved. No one asked him how, but he told us anyway. Apparently someone did an experiment with two boards and a light. One board had one hole and the other had two. The two boards were placed one in front of the other and a light was shone through the single hole. "Because it appeared through both holes on the second board," Stuart said, "proves that we can exist in two places at once." Ruth and I said nothing. I possibly had the same expression on my face as I had done after being told about the AM and PM muddle up. Ruth ended that conversation in her usual way by getting up and leaving the room and Stuart told me that as of midnight tonight the area is out of any state of emergency. I did not respond other than to say I was going to cook my dinner. But I caught his eye as I stood up and we both knew that he had told Rose she had been wrong. He's not a bad bloke. And he's not as daft as he makes out.

At midnight that night I heard fireworks going off as the village celebrated freedom and the following morning Ruth refused to speak to me. She slap-slapped her way into the kitchen, made her coffee and took it outside for the first time since I had been there.
Even Stuart was up and had his phone out, watching some app that showed him planes flying in and out of just about every country in the world. I was surprised to see him up before 11am but he seemed wide awake and cheerful. Normally it takes him a good hour to function in the mornings. I did cheerfully speak to Ruth and she was polite back but as I headed off to the river I couldn't help but wonder why Stuart was up so early. Maybe he was afraid Ruth and I would argue over the fact that Spain was now out of its state of emergency and Portugal still wouldn't open the land border.

I went to a spot by the river to sit and read because there was shade there and it was so hot in June. I sat and thought how nice it would be to just stay there. In the shade; surrounded by rocks and reeds; and with the only noise being that of the water and the birds. I could forget the rest of the world even existed. All I would need is shelter, food and fresh water. And internet.
Sad, but true, because I would need to know that my son is ok and I would need my books from the library. So a solar panel then, to charge my phone. I could only be a hermit if I could eat, drink, read and write.
Hummm, maybe not then!

But for a while it was a nice thought. The rest of the world could tear down status, ban books, films and even songs; people could all claim racial abuse from years ago and others could be too afraid to leave the house for fear of being called racist. The virus could spread because people have a 'right' not to wear a mask or wash their hands, and politicians could argue over who was going to fish where and who was going to ban who from what country; I would just sit by the river and read. I felt that as long as my son was alive, healthy and happy the rest of the world's population could Perch and Rotate!
Oh, it was such a peaceful and contented morning, but then I had to go back to the house.

Stuart and Ruth had spent the morning checking the internet and they had found two ways I could get back to Portugal. The first was a flight, direct, according to Ruth, but not until the 1st of July. She said there was no point in my leaving before that as there was no way I would get over the border before then anyway.
I asked for details of the flight and she got her phone out and found it then handed me the phone so I could see for myself. The flight left Alicante and landed in Madrid.
"That's only to Madrid," I said, handing back the phone.
"No it's not, it goes to Porto." She said. Standing next to me she put the phone on the table and pointed to the place names. Alicante and Porto. "See", she said, "Get on in Alicante and get off in Porto, so it's direct."
"So what's this?" I said, pointing to the 34 hour stopover in Madrid.

Stuart told me about trains. Apparently they were all sorted online and could be booked. I pointed out that I had tried to book just a few hours earlier and it wasn't possible, but he was adamant. So while I ate my lunch I checked it out. There were no planes with the company I had flown in with so I could not use my voucher. It was not yet possible to book the trains because they still didn't have the website sorted. Some timetables were there but others were not. I emailed the train company and was really surprised to get a response within an hour. After Google had translated it I found that trains were all running but couldn't be booked yet due to website problems. I was also told I would need a passport to travel so they knew exactly who was going where in case there was a problem. That was possibly the most welcome email I have ever had in my life.

I thought about booking a hotel and just sneaking out early in the morning without saying anything. But that would have been really rude.

So I booked a hotel and told them I was leaving on Tuesday.

The flowing day was very strained. Ruth spent most of it telling me that I should have got the flight to Porto and Stuart kept telling me that I was wasting money when I could have gone for £9.99.

"Why are you going to Badajoz when you could go straight to Portugal if you wait another week?" he asked.

"Because it's nearer to the village," I told him. "I can spend a week there, it'll be like a holiday and then I'll just get the bus on the first." He seemed to understand, but Ruth didn't.

"You're wasting money when you could have gone by plane much cheaper." Then, "Who did you fly out here with?"

I told her, "Iberia"

"So why don't you go back with them?"

"Because I want to go to Badajoz and they don't fly there."

"So go to Lisbon or Porto then."

I said nothing, she was making my brain hurt.

"You've lost your money, haven't you?"
"What?"
"The flight you had, the one they cancelled, you've lost the money."
"No, I paid with Avios and they gave me a credit note."
"With what?"
"Avios, or airmiles if you want to call them that."
"Phtt!"
I realised that she probably had no idea what I was talking about but didn't want to appear ignorant by asking. It briefly crossed my mind that I could tell her she doesn't just *appear* to be ignorant.
"So how are you getting to this place by the border?" I didn't blame her for that one, I was pretty sure I was pronouncing Badajoz totally wrong myself. I told her I was going by train; that I hadn't booked it but the trains were all running now so it would be fine.
"Where does the train go from?"
"I can get the train from here." I said, meaning the slab of concrete by the railway line behind the village that people jokingly refer to as a station.
She then informed me that local trains do not travel all the way across the country so I pointed out that local trains do go to Xativa. "From there I can get a train to Madrid and then one to Badajoz."
"That sounds a bit complicated," she said and I thought that leaving the house was complicated to Ruth. But I said nothing. She then asked how far the hotel was from the station and I told her about 3 kilometres.
"So how are you going to get there then?" she asked.
"Walk." I told her.
"Phtt, you'll never walk that far!"
I gave up.

I looked at Stuart to find him gently shaking his head with a pleading look in his eyes. I shrugged. I had no intention of taking the conversation further anyway. There was little point. I was reminded of the saying about playing chess with a pigeon, where the pigeon hasn't got the brain power to know what to do, but struts about over the board as if he won the game anyway.

That evening, as I said goodnight, Stuart asked what time I would be leaving in the morning. "About 7," I said. "The train goes at 7.30."
Stuart then said he would walk with me to the station and I was pleased. I told him it wasn't really necessary but that I would be grateful for the company. I was also grateful for the fact that Ruth stayed quiet. I really didn't want her company; I didn't even want her to get out of bed until after I had left. But she did.

Just as I was getting my bag done up and Stuart was checking that I had enough water and coffee and coins and masks and sandwiches, I smelled that 'just crawled out of a pit' smell that wafts around people who don't wash much and sleep heavy. Thankfully she simply walked passed and went to the kitchen. I proved to Stuart that I had my passport and my phone and I double checked my room, as instructed, to make sure I hadn't left anything and came back to find her at the breakfast/dining room table.
"We'd better go," said Stuart.
"Yep, Thanks for everything Ruth, you've been great." I lied.
"Bye." She said, without taking her eyes from her phone.

Stuart and I walked to the station chatting about all sorts of things. We chatted as we waited on the slab of concrete until the train came. Then I gave him a hug and said, "Thank you. I really mean that. Thank you so much for everything."

Then I put on my mask and got on the train without a backward glance. I found a seat and sat down, leaning back into the seat as the train pulled away. It was 40 degrees C and I was wearing a cotton face mask that I wore all that day as I travelled right across Spain.
I had never felt so free.

Printed in Poland
by Amazon Fulfillment
Poland Sp. z o.o., Wrocław